I0580272

It's Like Living in a dream

By

Mervyn J. Edwards

Copyright © 2025

Dedication

All In A Dream is dedicated to my late mother who passed away before I had a chance to prove her wrong.

Many years ago when I first started writing _All In A Dream_ she told me it was nothing but filth and dis-owned me as her son for writing such filth.

Well dear my mother it might be filth in your eyes but in others it isn't so "Rest In Peace" and if I could send you a copy of it I would.

Acknowledgement

All the names contained within this book and the place where Jake the handyman worked are purely fictional and are not the names of real people or a place that Dr Edwards knows. As he has stated this book was written from a continuous dream nothing more.

All In A Dream is not a copy-write by any means, it is solely the work of the author himself.

The five main people within the story and are strictly from the imagination of Dr Edwards's dream nothing else and they are:

Jake Woodman the handyman

April Conway the daughter

Lexie Conway the wife

Adam Conway the husband

Brook Cambridge who is Lexie's best friend

The name of the place where Jake worked is called _'Loin's Den'_

M. J. Edwards

Acknowledgement And Thanks

To all my dear friends back in Australia who wanted to know the ending here it is. It took many years for it to go to print but the wait is worthwhile in the end.

To all those who said it wouldn't get published and it was nothing but pure garbage this is to prove you all wrong.

Table of Contents

Dedication iii

Acknowledgement iv

Acknowledgement And Thanks v

Prologue 1

About The Author 3

Chapter One 5

Chapter Two 7

Chapter Three 11

Chapter Four 14

Chapter Five 17

Chapter Six 21

Chapter Seven 28

Chapter Eight 31

Chapter Nine 37

Chapter Ten 43

Chapter Eleven 50

Chapter Twelve 59

Chapter Thirteen 63

Chapter Fourteen 67

M. J. Edwards

Prologue

April placed a floatable deck chair into the pool and laid back to catch some early morning rays while floating around. As she laid there catching the early morning sun rays, she closed her eyes and thought about Jake lying there in his hospital bed.

Oh how she longed to be with him during the holidays, she gave a sigh as she nodded of the sleep. Her dream was to be of her man and how it would be like to make love to him and pictured Jake the following way. A young lad of 22 and built like a brick shit house! He worked as a stripper by night and a handy man by day at a very large country estate. One day while Jake was cleaning the pool he decided to take a swim, thinking that everyone had gone out for the day. Jake always had his tape recorder playing while he worked. So as he started to undress, he decided to dance as if he was performing in front of a large crowd. Little did he know that April the Boss's daughter was watching from her bedroom window!

As Jake was dancing to the beat of his music, April watched as his fingers moved up and down his shirt undoing the buttons as he went. As Jake danced to the beat of his music April was hypnotized by his swaying body that she too was swaying to his music as well. The moment Jake's shirt hit the deck of the pool, April dropped the cup that she was holding, the more Jake moved, the more turned on little April became. April watched as Jake's hands started moving down towards his shorts. As she watched, unknown to what she was doing, April soon had her hands rubbing her sweet little mound.

Then in a flash Jake's shorts were gone exposing his skimpy G-String jocks exposing the cutest bum that she had ever seen. On seeing this inviting sight, April was unable to control her emotions anymore and let out a squeal. As Jake continued to dance; he moved his G-String jocks up and down exposing and recovering his large ever-growing dick. The moment young April saw Jake's dick hanging free in the breeze she knew that she had to have it between her legs. Knowing that her parents would not be home for hours, she decided to join Jake in the pool. Jake laid back looking up at the sun and didn't hear April enter the pool from the other end,

1

because his music was still belting out its lively little tune. All of a sudden he felt a warm set of lips engulf his swollen cock. Jake was back in the land of the living with the biggest fright of his life.

Young April just smiled and took it once again into her mouth. After a while, Jake drew April to his mouth slipping his tongue into her mouth. With that April wrapped her legs around his waist so Jake could insert his throbbing cock into April's hot little box. April gave a moan as his large cock entered her tight little virgin pussy for the first time. April whispers into Jake's ear saying, "take it gentle honey it's my first time." With that Jake lifted April from the pool and laid her back spreading her legs, and then borrowed his tongue into her very hot little muffin.

The moment Jake's tongue entered her sweet little pussy; April sat up to see what Jake was doing to her sweet little pussy. Jake then shifted his tongue and worked on her button, the moment Jake's tongue hit her button she had to have him inside her right now. She helped Jake out of the pool, where Jake laid her back down and was just about to enter the hottest little pussy he ever had the pleasure to enter. When the sound of her mother yelling from the kitchen, window made April fall into the pool bringing her back to reality.

About The Author

Dr Mervyn J Edwards is a psychologist and has written a book called _'How To Become An Academic Genius Using Plus One'_ and _'The Mind From A Different Perspective'_. In his books he talks about how to control your dreams and _'All In A Dream'_ was written many years ago when Dr Edwards was in his late 20's by controlling a dream which lasted for 8 nights.

All In A Dream is a romance novel and full of sexual experiences throughout written when he was unemployed back in Australia. He is now a university English Professor in China.

The scene for this romance novel takes place on a very big country estate something like you see in the movies.

When you read this book Dr Edwards advises to get the most from this book is that you make yourself into one of the people within the story.

Some of Dr Edwards's friends who were having material problems came to him seeking advice on how to improve their sex life. All Dr Edwards did was hand then the prologue and the first few chapters of this book and said _"read this it will give you all the help you need"_.

Shortly afterwards his friends came back to him thanking him for giving it to them saying, their sex life has become better that ever since reading it and want to read the rest of the book.

Now not being the sort of book that appeals to many publishers it has stayed on his computer for the past 20 or so years along with many other books he has written.

If you want to learn how to control your dreams, then it would pay you to purchase his other two books. _'How To Become An Academic Genius Using Plus One'_ has just been published and _'The Mind From A Different Perspective'_ is due to be published sometime in the next year.

Both of Dr Edwards's books are psychology books relating to the mind a far cry from this book but well worthwhile reading just the same.

It's Like Living in a dream

If you have any question on how to improve your life or any sexual problems you might have you can contact him by email at <u>2714forever@gmail.com</u>

Chapter One

A young man by the name of Jake Woodman was out of work for 6 months, things were starting to get on top of him. He was only able to obtain little odd jobs from time to time, but he knew that he was destined for bigger and brighter things. As he nodded off to sleep he was dreaming that he was employed as a handyman at a very large country estate. He was weeding the garden in the middle of the turnaround, when he heard a car coming up the drive. Jake swivelled around to see who it was, it was Alexis; but known as Lexie the boss's wife. _"Jake would you be able you make sure the pool is lean ready for tonight, April is having a party in there"_ she replied.

"OK Mrs Conway I'll get to it straight away"_ Jake replied. While she was talking to Jake, Lexie noticed the bulge in the front of her handyman's shorts.

Unknown to Jake, his left testicle was hanging free in the breeze. On seeing the exposed flesh, Lexie commented on his shorts pointing to his crutch saying, _"that doesn't look like a bad pair you have there"_ and drove off. Jake was a bit stunned and sat there a bit puzzled as to what Lexie meant about not having a bad pair, and then he looked down and saw what she was talking about and began to blush. Jake gathered up his gardening tools and headed off to the pool to start to carry out the orders that were given to him by his eye balling boss's wife. Meanwhile Lexie had gone to the room and changed into her skimpiest pair of bikinis and waited for Jake to start cleaning the pool. The moment he started to clean the pool Lexie entered and was heading straight for the deck chair saying, _"mind if I watch"_ dropping her robe to the ground.

"No not at all" Jake replied turning around. In doing that he was to see the boss's wife in the smallest pair of bikinis he had ever seen. This was to make his eyes light up, like a pair of headlights on full beam as he saw her gorgeous body was being revealed.

Just before Jake was about to finish for the day, Adam (Lexie's husband) asked if he was able to attend April's party tonight. Sorry was his reply for he was meeting someone at the _Lion's Den_. He did not let on to his new employers that he worked as stripper there at night to earn some extra cash, for the fear of losing his daytime job at the estate.

The next day as Jake was cleaning up the mess from the party, he noticed young April lying in the pool on a floatable deck chair. Thinking that she was asleep, he stood there and admired her beautiful body. Knowing that Jake was standing there watching her; April opened her legs wide revealing the outline of her beautiful little mound. With Jake's cock now bulging to be let loose, he turned and walked away to relieve the pressure. After Jake had left, April laughed for she knew where he was heading.

Later that night, Jake decided to go for a swim, as the night air was hotter than normal. As he paddled around in the pool minding his own business, April was watching his muscular body from her room. On seeing the body, which she was able to arouse earlier, but this time it was almost naked, she decided to take it one step further. April told her mother that she was going for a swim and changed into her bikini and headed off to work her magic on the man in the pool. But by the time April had gotten to the pool Jake was gone.

"Oh shit!" April blurted out after finding out that Jake had left before she had a chance to do anything, so she left there in her own little fantasy. But unknown to April, Jake had gone to sleep and was dreaming of that hot little pussy he was earlier in the day.

Chapter Two

On entering the kitchen, the first person Jake saw was sweet little April. At that moment, the biggest smile came across his face remembering his dream about her hot little cunt sitting there upon his tongue. On seeing his broad smile, April asked Jake what he was smiling about. _"Ah nothing you want to know"_ as he headed for the fridge.

"Come on tell" April demanded, as she chased Jake around the kitchen, only to be saved by Adam and Lexie walking in. April said _"I'll get it out of you later"_.

"Get what out of you later" her father asked inquisitively.

"Jake is hiding something from me dad and he won't tell me, and I intend to find out" as she strutted off to her room.

"Please excuse my daughter Jake; she's a lot like her mother, she wants to know everything" and leaning over kissing Lexie on the cheek.

"There is a list of things I would like you to do today for me" pointing to the bench.

"The place is in a bit of a mess, our other gardener didn't return after he won a large sum of money on the pokies" Adam said with a hit of anger in his voice.

"She'll be cool Mr Conway; I'll have your place ship shape in no time at all you'll see" Jake replied as he hoed into his breaky.

"OK the first thing I would like you to do is the hedge around the court yard of the pool" Adam replied looking at them through the kitchen window. On hearing the pool mentioned, Jake choked on his breaky as he remembered his dream about shagging young April in there last night.

"You OK!" Lexie asked slapping him on the back. Jake nodded as the smile came back to his face. With that April came back into the kitchen asking her father if Jake could get the leaves out of the pool first thing because she was dying for a swim.

It's Like Living in a dream

Jake choked again as the pool was mentioned again, getting an even bigger response from Lexie saying; _"You sure you're all right"_. Jake gave another nod as he put his bowl in the sink.

Seeing this pool subject is making Jake choke, Adam turned to Jake saying, _"Are you afraid of the water or can't you swim"_ looking quite concerned.

"No I'm not afraid of the water; and I am a very good swimmer. It's just seems funny that's what I had a dream about last night", little did they know that he was fucking the arse off their daughter at the time. On hearing that, all 4 began to laugh causing Jake to choke once more. Adam replied saying; _"We better leave the pool alone before we kill the poor lad"_ heading out the door for work. Lexie asked April if she wanted to go into town with to do some shopping, no thanks she replied, for she wanted to catch up on thing here. _"Very well dear I'll see you around 4 o'clock then"_.

"OK mother, you have a nice day" came a voice from somewhere within the house.

Meanwhile, Jake had left to tidy up the pool area that nearly killed him at breakfast. Not knowing that he will be left alone with his spunky little April, his lover in his hottest sexual dream of his life. Jake had finished tiding up the pool area and was looking around to see if anyone was watching him, for he was going to take a quick dip before finishing his work. As he looked towards the house, he noticed young April getting changed in front of the window in her room. On seeing her movements he entered into yet another sexual dream about this hot little school. He was cleaning the pool and in a world of his own when she entered saying, _"that's not a bad arse you have there"_ when she spoke it was too caught off balance making him fell into the pool.

"HOLY SHIT"! Jake blurted out as he surfaced from under the water, then apologized saying, _"sorry Miss April you scared the shit right out of me"_ apologizing once more. Adding, _"you don't have a bad arse yourself"_.

By this time April saw in a big fit of laughter saying, _"you can just call me April like mum and dad and not Miss April OK"_.

"How much longer will you be cleaning the pool Jake"? She replied still laughing.

"If I didn't fall into the pool I would be finished by now" Jake replied. With that April dropped her robe to the ground and dived in leaving Jake there with his mouth wide open on seeing her beautiful body.

"You better close your mouth before you catch some flies" April chuckled as she swam to the other side. Jake could feel his dick starting to rise as he watched her swim across to the other side saying the April as she reached the other side, _"I better go and finish the other jobs that your dad wants done"_.

As Jake turned around to get out of the pool April swam back across getting closer and closer to what she knew was a red-hot hard cock just waiting to be let loose. Just as Jake was about to exit, April grabbed him turning him back around. With a smile April reached down taking hold of his throbbing dick saying, _"oh my goodness, what do we have here"_?

With Jake now starting to sweat profusely, he began to tremble as April unleashed his dick from his shorts. _"Hum what am I going to do with this"_ looking at him smiling.

"I know" she said as she went under the water. With April's lips firmly around his swollen dick, all that he could do was lean back and enjoy. Gasping for air, April surfaced being pulled straight to Jake's lips where they stayed for quite a while.

Meanwhile unknown to Jake, while April was under the water she had removed her bikini briefs. April's hot little moot was now dripping from her love juices as she wrapped her legs around his waist. Jake was able to insert his throbbing cock into her aching little twat. The moment he entered her sweet little vagina, April moaned with delight as Jake's cock was inserted. Wanting to taste her forbidden fruits, he lifted her up and placed her on the side of the pool. As April sat there legs wide apart, Jake embedded his tongue into her tunnel of love. April's body was moving with delight as Jake worked on her precious little love button. The faster Jake's tongue went, the faster April moved. All of a sudden, April let out a little squeal, as she let her love juices flow over Jake's tongue.

It's Like Living in a dream

Knowing that April had reached her first orgasm, Jake laid her down and ascended from the pool with April saying, _"Oh fuck honey I want you now"_! With that Jake inserted his dick once more into her love-starved tunnel of love, where they reached one of their best moments, in what was to turn out to be one the hottest romances ever seen at the estate. Now Jake was brought back to reality with the sound of the pool gate opening and the sound of April's voice saying, _"Jake are you finished yet"_.

"Yes April, I'm finished" replied picking up the hedger and leaving her all alone.

Chapter Three

Back at the office, Adam arranged for Lexie to meet him there so he could take her to a business luncheon. About an hour into the luncheon, Adam started to get horny and started feeling Lexie up under the table. Brook, who was Lexie's best friend was Lexie squirming with delight and knew exactly what the pair were up to. Brook became excited at the thought of what her friends were doing that she too was getting by the signals that Lexie was giving to Adam. Adam whispered into Lexie's ear something and the two of them bit their fair wells and headed back to Adam's office, leaving the rest to the bull shit that was going on around the table. Brook knew exactly where they were heading and gave her apologies and left as well.

In the elevator, and out of the sight of prying eyes; Lexie lent on the wall so Adam could give her a sample of what was to come. Before Adam could tuck his dick back into his pants, the elevator doors sprang open exposing the randy couple. Lucky no one was at the opened doors waiting to enter giving Adam time to put his love tool away before they left for his office. As Adam turned around from closing the door to his office, his horny wife already had her blouse off exposing her rock hard tits. After caressing, sucking and nibbling on each tit, Adam dropped to his knees taking Lexie's knickers with him. With Adam buried between Lexie's legs, and Adam forgetting to lock the door, Brook entered. The stunned pair didn't know what to say as they saw Brook standing there looking at Adam as he slowly got to his feet. They were even more shocked when Brook asked if she could join in as she dropped her dress to the floor.

Adam looked at Lexie and getting the nod they both took Brook by the hand and lead her over to the couch. Over on the couch, Adam laid on his back while Lexie mounted his cock while Brook sat on his face. After a while the two ladies changed positions and commenced caressing and kissing each other once more. The three were to enjoy each other's company, well into the afternoon. After a while, Brook realized what she had done. Apologized for her intrusion she ran for the door dressing as she went, only to be confronted by Lexie. _"It's OK love, I didn't mine you getting shafted by Adam, and I know Adam didn't mind either"_ looking over at him as they all proceeded to dress each other. Lexie left Adam clean up their love juices that were all over the couch and walked Brook to the elevator. Brook apologized once more for intruding in on them only to be given a kiss saying, _"we'll do lunch again tomorrow at my place"_ as the elevator doors closed.

The next day was here before Brook knew it, now Brook was hesitant about meeting Lexie at her place for lunch today. Closing her eyes, Brook was remembering the day before. She was being screwed by her best friend's husband right in front of her very eyes, knowing full well that it would put a strain on their relationship. Brook was going to call and cancel the planned luncheon with Lexie fearing a hostile confrontation on her arrival. Lexie had forgotten that she had to take April to the bus station today, so she yelled out to Jake and asked him to do it for her. _"Jake would you be a honey and escort April into town to catch her bus, I forgot that I am meeting Mrs Cambridge here for lunch"_.

"OK Mrs Conway, I'll be there in a minute, I just have to change first" he hallowed back at her. As Jake and April were heading down the drive, Brook was coming up and looking quite nervous.

"Hello Mrs Cambridge" April yelled as they passed each other on the drive.

"Off to school again I see; I'll see you again when you come back home then my dear" driving up to the house.

"GOD WHO WAS THAT SPUNK"! Jake remarked veering off the drive way.

"That's mum's best friend Brook Cambridge, she lost her husband last year in a boating accident and she often comes over to see mum" April replied.

"SHE IS ONE FOXY CHICK" responding to April's information. Only straightening up the car after getting a slap from April yelling; _"Put your eyes back in your head and watch where you're going"_.

On their arrival at the bus station April turns to Jake saying, _"Jake"_.

"Yes young April, did you call me" Jake responding to her request.

"You see that girl over there, the one with the long blonde hair looking over this way" getting a nod from him.

"Well would you mind if I ask you to give me a kiss just before I get on the bus and say that you can hardly wait for me to return"?

Looking kind of shy for asking her question. Well the stunned looking Jake replied, _"It will be my pleasure"_ for he had dreamed of this moment twice now.

"Great that will piss the bitch off" April chuckled as he put his arm around her waist as he escorted her to the bus. When April and Jake reached Donna who was leaning against the bus with her nose in the air, Jake turned to April and gave her the biggest kiss he had ever given anyone. With that April grabbed Jake by the dick saying, _"I'll have this when I come back home"_ making his eyes light up and his cock stand to attention. As April let go of his throbbing dick and threw her arms around his neck giving him another kiss. All Donna could do was just stared with her mouth wide open as she gazed at the size of the bulge in the front of Jake's shorts. April looks at Donna saying; _"That's mine bitch so get your fucking eyes of his cock"_ as she disappeared into the bus. Hot and horny, Jake headed for home wondering if April meant what she said about his dick. With a massive hard on, Jake had a hard time concentrating on his driving as he remembered what April said over and over.

Chapter Four

Back at the estate, Lexie and Brook were having a cup of tea. With Brook not knowing if Lexie was mad at her for banging her husband, she remained very quiet. Lexie, seeing that Brook was very distant put her cup down on the table. Walking up behind Brook saying, _"did you enjoy yourself yesterday with my husband"_ putting her hand on her shoulder. The moment Lexie's hand touched her shoulder Brook dropped her cup spilling tea everywhere. But before she could answer Lexie's question, Lexie's hand was creasing one of her tit making her even more nervous. As Lexie gently creased her nice firm breast, she whispered in her ear saying, _"I really didn't mind you getting fucked by Adam yesterday, for it gave me a chance to explore your body"_ giving her a kiss on the cheek. In saying that, Lexie started undoing the buttons on Brook's blouse releasing her softly rounded breasts. On seeing those gorgeous tits once more, Lexie placed one of them in her mouth once more. Now knowing what Lexie had on her mind, Brook joined in and started creasing Lexie's rock hard tits as well.

Jake was to arrive home a few moments later, only to find the pair the pair enjoying each other on the bearskin rug in the lounge room. With his eyes bulging at the sight of those two gorgeous bodies rolling around on the floor, his dick was now busting to be flogged. With all that has happened in the last few hours, Jake had to release to pressure now building in his ball and had to expose his love juices to the world.

After the girls had finished what they were doing, they went out on to the porch with another cup of tea. Brook turns to Lexie saying, _"who is that young spunk you have doing your gardens"_.

"He is our new handyman Jake Woodman; he has been with us for a week now, he started the day of April's birthday. The other bastard didn't return from his weekend off, he apparently suppose too have won a fortune on the pokies. We were lucky to get him on such short notice and he has been a real gem so far".

"Boy he has a cute arse on him and that body! What wouldn't I give the have someone like Jake sharing my bed" Brook said sheepishly.

"Jake can you come here for a minute please; there is someone I would like to meet" yelled Lexie waving at him from the porch.

"OK I'm coming" he replied dusting himself off.

-"I hope not"_ Brook giggling to Lexie.

"Jake, this is Brook Cambridge" as Lexie started to introduce her friend only to be cut off by Jake.

"Yes I know who you are Mrs Cambridge, April told me earlier" he replied.

"Sorry to hear about you old man" Jake replied in a soft voice shaking her hand.

"It's OK honey" replied Brook giving him a little kiss on the cheek.

"Jake, do you think you would be able to help Brook from time to time looking after her place" Lexie asked.

"She'll be OK Mrs Conway; I'll have both your places looking great in no time, you'll see".

"Will you stop calling me Mrs Conway it makes me sound old, my name is Lexie and this is Brook" Lexie said pointing her finger.

"That'll be all thanks Jake; you can go and finish what you were doing now" Lexie said with a smile.

"OK Mrs Conway". Lexie's eyes lit up with rage on hearing those words again. _"Ah got you there Lexie"_ Jake grinned as he turned and walked away. Just as he turned and started walking away, Brook grabbed him by the arse saying, _"Nice bum you have there Jake"_. Jake looked back saying; _"you have a very nice one as well"_ giving it a pat as he walked pass!

"You shouldn't tease the young lad like that dear" Lexie said as she put her arm around Brook's waist.

"I couldn't help myself; he really does have a very cute arse" Brook replied looking quite serious. With that remark Lexie asked Brook if she wanted to stay there tonight, for Adam had to go out of town on business for a couple of days.

"I'd love to honey, it gets lonely over there by myself but in what bed will I be sleeping in" Brook asked cheekily. With that Lexie gave Brook a kiss on the cheek.

As darkness fell, the two horny little devils retired it the main bedroom where the undressed each other ready for a shower. While Lexie was feeling around in Brook's blonde tuff of hair, Brook was doing the same in Lexie's auburn mound of fluff as they deeply embraced before they showered. In the shower they worked on each other's body, caressing each other's breasts and inserting their fingers deep inside each other's hot little vaginas. Working each other up to frenzy as you reached what was to be their first orgasm for the night.

Being nice and refreshed after their shower and being as horny as hell; Brook laid Lexie onto her red satin sheets spreading her legs wide. As Brook's tongue moved in on Lexie's hot little button, Lexie begged her lover to climb onto the bed. Both of them were now moving as one as their clitorises were being stimulated by each other, their vaginas are now starting to over flow with the sweet nectar of one another. Their climaxes were obtained simultaneously, their moans, squeals and sighs echoed in the still night air.

Chapter Five

The next morning as Jake was in the kitchen having breakfast, Lexie and Brook walked in giggling and smiling like two little school-girls. _"Did you two have a good night sleep ladies" he replied looking up from the table.

"Yes"; they replied as they joined Jake at the breakfast table. As Jake finished, was about to head out the kitchen door but stopped in the middle and turned back to the two little lovers. _"Lexie, I couldn't help seeing both of your beautiful bodies in the lounge room yesterday"_ as he again turned to walk out the door.

"What did you see in the lounge room yesterday Jake"? Brook asked with a stunned look upon her face stopping him in his tracks again.

"Well I was weeding the garden, when I saw you two making out on the lounge floor" Jake replied with a smile, leaving the two of them gazing at each other with their mouth wide open. From that day on they met at Brook's place, out of the sight of those peeping eyes.

Two weeks have passed since Jake saw Brook and Lexie on the lounge floor of the estate. Lexie told Jake, that Brook was coming over to take him back to her place to do some work for her. When Brook arrived she wearing a pair of shorts that barely covered the cheeks of her bum. Making, both Lexie's eyes and Jake's eyes light with desire.

"Are you ready to go Jake"? Brook asked beckoning him towards her car.

"One minute, I'll go and change first" Jake yelled back. Brook turned to Lexie and with a sheepish grin and whispered; _"I'll see you tonight"_ as she headed down the drive to pick up Jake. _"You'll be over there until about 4 o'clock, that's not too late for you to be away is it Jake" Brook asked.

"No I don't think it should be a problem for me" he replied.

On their arrival at Brook's estate, Jake couldn't see what he had to mow as the lawn looked all right to him, but it wasn't his place to argue with the bosses. _"The first thing I would like you to do is to shift some furniture in some of the bedrooms up stairs. So the cleaners can get in behind them and give the room a bloody good clean; and then you will be able to do the outside chores OK"_!

"You're the boss" Jake replied, as he was led up the stairs to the bedrooms, glancing back at the lawn once more.

"We'll start in the main bedroom" as Brook opened up the door. _"Right the first thing I want you to do is take your clothes off"_ as she pushed him onto the bed face first.

"Brook do you realize what you're saying, Mr Conway will have my arse if he found out that I screwed his wife's best friend; And what would Lexie say, knowing that I was screwing her lover instead of working" as he tried to get off the bed.

"Just do as you're told and take your clothes off before I rip them off" as she was going for his belt. As Brook was undoing his belt, Jake proceeded to fumble with his zipper.

"Let me do it for you" as she took his hand away from his zip. Brook then proceeded to release his swiftly growing muscle; her awaiting eyes couldn't believe the size of it as it started to stand to attention. _"Oh dreary me, what can I do with that"_ bending down giving it a kiss as Jake lifted his arse so Brook could remove his jeans. While Brook was removing his jeans; Jake removed Brook's top. With his jeans gone and her top missing, Jake grabbed her pulling Brook to the bed beside him. Brook laid back all innocent as Jake removed his shirt before he started on the rest of Brook's unwanted clothing.

On removing the rest of Brook's unwanted clothing, Jake knelt down beside the bed and started kissing his way up to her blonde tuff of hair. As he kissed his way slowly up to her pussy, his hands found their way to her nice firm breasts. Jake had almost found his target when Brook spread her legs wide exposing her forbidden as Jake's tongue hit its mark. Jake knew that there was no turning back now as he proceeded to work her clitoris. From there Jake moved up towards her nice firm tits, kissing Brook ever so slowly as he went. On reaching her nice firm tit with erected nipples, Jake places the left one into his mouth while gently squeezing the right. With Brook's left breast in his mouth, Jake gently nibbled and sucked on her shivering nipple while gently squeezing the other. Brook dug her finger nails into Jake's back as she moaned sighed as he moved his way up towards my mouth.

"Oh yes"! Brook mumbled softly as Jake's dick frond its mark. _"Fuck me Jake, fuck me"_ Brook pleaded as she was reaching her first orgasm. Only to have Jake withdraw his cock from her soaking wet tunnel of joy, only so he can reinsert his tongue.

"You fucking big tease" Brook blurted out, as Jake buried his head as hard as he could between her legs.

Rolling and whinnying around on the bed as Jake manoeuvred his tongue even faster as Brook's orgasm was reached. _"Fucking hell Jake I can't take any more of this, I want your cock inside me"_ as her hips moved like pistons up and down. With that, Jake rolled her over and started manoeuvring his tongue around her arse while he caressed her nipples from behind. With her tits already hard and her nipples well excited, Brook screamed as a bigger and more powerful climax was reached. Once Brook had reached her second climax, he rolled her back over and placed his dripping cock into her even wetter twat, where he over flowed it with his juices. Oncc hc had finished spewing his white sticky load between her legs, Jake held her in his arms while they both savoured the moments of lust.

After about an hour, Jake went for a shower leaving Brook to sigh away in what was the best sexual experience of her life. When Jake had redressed, he headed off down stairs and began to fix them both lunch. Jake was soon joined by Brook who was only wearing her blouse and knickers. Brook went over to and wrapped her arms around Jake's waist from behind giving him a big hug, then kissed him in the middle of the back saying; _"that was the first time anyone has ever made me feel like that"_ turning him around and kissing him once more.

Jake asked _"did you get me over here to mow your lawn and move furniture or was it just so you could get the arse fucked out of you"_?

"What do you think" laying a big passionate kiss upon his lips!

Coming up for air, Jake replied, _"you horny little bitch, what would Lexie say if she finds out that I was over here fucking the arse off her lover instead of mowing your lawn"_.

"But you did mow my lawn didn't you" grabbing him by his cock. _"Besides she has Adam to satisfy her when I'm not there and I think it's only fair that I have someone else as well"_ giving his balls a gentle kneed. _"Well I suppose I'd better get you back, your boss is due home"_ Brook remarked. _"But before I do"_ dropping to her knees to release his fast growing dick once more, _"I would like another taste of this fucking great cock of yours"_ talking it in her mouth again. With that, Jake brought Brook from her knees and bent her over the kitchen table. Taking down her knickers, he placed his erected cock into her again and slowly fucked away until their love juices entwined yet again.

Lexie greeted them on their arrival and said to Jake, _"I hope she didn't work you too hard did she"_.

"Only as hard as any woman would have" turning towards Brook. Then adding, _"If you don't mind Lexie, I think I'll go and have a shower and call it a day"_.

"Go on love, I think you deserve it after the day you just put in" Brook winked.

"Yes that's OK honey; I'll see you for supper" as Jake headed for his room.

Chapter Six

Over the next few days leading up to the school holidays, Jake was busy getting the yard in Mickey Mouse condition, For he figured if all his work was done, he would be able to spend more time April. Jake was making sure that the pool was spic and span; because he knew that the moment April came home she would be heading straight for it. He imagined her walking into the pool area in her skimpy bikinis and dropping her robe like she did the first time he ever saw her. Jake couldn't wait to find out whether April meant what she said the day when she got on the bus.

The day before April was due home; Jake mind was not on the job at hand. All he could think of was April's word, that's mine! Pointing to his crutch as he was trimming the rose bushes! All of a sudden, Jake let out a yell as he stood there with a thorn from one of the bushes in his leg. _"BLOODY BITCH"_! He cried as he bent over to pull it out, only to be pricked by another thorn in the eye. Lexie came running to Jake's aid after hearing his cry for help, on seeing him bleeding from the eye; she drove him straight to the hospital. The doctor took one look at his eye and told Lexie that her gardener had to be admitted for observations, to see if there was any damage done to the pupil?

After Jake was admitted, it was nearly time to pick up April from the bus terminal. Lexie bid her farewells to her wounded gardener with a big passionate kiss and went to fetch her daughter. As the bus drove into the terminal, April got all excited at the possibility of her intended lover being there waiting for her.

As the bus came to a halt, April was the first one off. Running inside to be in the waiting arms of her would be lover, only to have her heart sink at the sight of her mother and not Jake. _"How was your trip home darling"_ she asked giving her a kiss on the cheek.

"It was OK I guess" answering with a depress voice.

"Well let's get your bags; I want to check on Jake" Lexie said hurrying her daughter along.

"Where is he, has something happened to him mum"? April inquired.

It's Like Living in a dream

"I had to put him the hospital about an hour ago" Lexie replied grabbing one of her bags. By this time, April was getting historical, wanting to know more. _"What's wrong with him mum"_? April inquiring again as she started to cry!

-"Not much honey"_ but before her mother could explain she was interrupted by her daughter saying; _"there must be something wrong for him to be in there"_ April questing her mother's answer.

"Well if you let me finish, I will tell you all right" as they headed out of the terminal.

On the way to the hospital, Lexie explained how Jake was to be in the there. When they reached the hospital they were told that he was resting and could not be disturbed. _"Pigs arse"_! April yelled as she headed into his ward.

"Please excuse my daughter; she has had a long trip home from school by bus" Lexie explained following her into the ward. April took hold of Jake's hand as he laid there sleeping turning to her mother, _"do you think he will be all right, he isn't going too loose his eye is he"_?

"I don't think so", as she gave her daughter a cuddle. _"Come on, let's leave him sleep. We'll come and see him tomorrow, he'll be awake then"_. April started to sob again, as she gave his hand a kiss before letting it go.

All the way home, April sat there staring out the window not saying anything. All she could think about was Jake lying there in a bloody hospital bed, ruining the night that she had planned on her way home from school. On their arrival home, April went straight to her room where she sobbed herself to sleep. When April didn't come down for supper when she was called, Lexie went up to April's room, only to find her daughter sound asleep. Pulling up the covers, Lexie gave her daughter a kiss on the forehead and went back down to the kitchen. _"Is April OK honey"_ Adam inquiring about his daughter.

-"Yes, she's sleeping; the trip home wasn't a good one"_ Lexie replied.

The next morning, April was up bright and early and very eager to get going to the hospital to see how Jake was. _"What are you doing up so early honey"_ Lexie asked with a yawn.

"I'm getting ready to go in and see Jake" April replied.

"You won't be able to see him for another 3 hours honey" her mother replied with another yawn.

"THREE HOURS! What am I going to do for another three hours"? April moaned _"I'm not tired"_ she went on to say.

"Well go for a swim then, that will pass away some of the time, I'm going back to bed" Lexie said with another yawn.

_"OK"_! April grumbled as she stomped of too her room to change.

April placed a floatable deck chair into the pool and laid back to catch some early morning rays while floating around. As she laid there catching the early morning sun rays, she closed her eyes and thought about Jake lying there in his hospital bed. Oh how she longed to be with him during the holidays, she gave a sigh as she nodded of the sleep. Her dream was to be of her man and how it would be like to make love to him and remembered Jake the following way.

A young lad of 22 and built like a brick shit house! He worked as a stripper by night and a handyman by day at a very large country estate. One day while Jake was cleaning the pool he decided to take a swim, thinking that everyone had gone out for the day. Jake always had his tape recorder playing while he worked. So as he started to undress, he decided to dance as if he was performing in front of a large crowd.

Little did he know that April the boss's daughter was watching from her bedroom window! As Jake was dancing to the beat of his music, April watched as his fingers moved up and down his shirt undoing the buttons as he went. As Jake danced to the beat of his music April was hypnotized by his swaying body that she too was swaying to his music as well. The moment Jake's shirt hit the deck of the pool, April dropped the cup that she was holding, the more Jake moved, the more turned on little April became. April watched as Jake's hands started moving down towards his shorts. As she watched, unknown to what she was doing, April soon had her hands rubbing her sweet little mound.

In a flash Jake's shorts were gone exposing his skimpy G-String jocks exposing the cutest bum that she had ever seen. On seeing this inviting sight, April was unable to control her emotions anymore and let out a squeal. As Jake continued to dance; he moved his G-String jocks up and down exposing and recovering his large ever-growing dick. The moment young April saw Jake's dick hanging free in the breeze she knew that she had to have it between her legs. Knowing that her parents would not be home for hours, she decided to join Jake in the pool. Jake laid back looking up at the sun and didn't hear April enter the pool from the other end, because his music was still belting out its lively little tune. All of a sudden he felt a warm set of lips engulf his swollen cock. Jake was back in the land of the living with the biggest fright of his life. Young April just smiled and took it once again into her mouth.

After a while, Jake drew April to his mouth slipping his tongue into her mouth. With that April wrapped her legs around his waist so Jake could insert his throbbing cock into April's hot little box. April gave a moan as his large cock entered her tight little virgin pussy for the first time. April whispers into Jake's ear saying, "take it gentle honey it's my first time." With that Jake lifted April from the pool and laid her back spreading her legs, and then borrowed his tongue into her very hot little muffin.

The moment Jake's tongue entered her sweet little pussy; April sat up to see what Jake was doing to her sweet little pussy. Jake then shifted his tongue and worked on her button, the moment Jake's tongue hit her button she had to have him inside her right now. She helped Jake out of the pool, where Jake laid her back down and was just about to enter the hottest little pussy he ever had the pleasure to enter. When the sound of her mother yelling from the kitchen, window made April fall into the pool bringing her back to reality.

"Are you coming to see Jake" Lexie yelled as April dragged herself out of the pool.

"What time is it"? April replied reaching for her towel.

"It's almost 10 o'clock; we'll leave as soon as you're dressed if you want" Lexie hollowed back.

"I'll only be 5 minutes" April said running past her mother.

On their arrival at the hospital, April didn't even wait for the car to stop before she had the door open. "Just wait until I park the car April! So we can both go in together" Lexie said in a stern voice.

"Ah mum"! April moaned slamming the door.

With-in 10 minutes, both Lexie and April were in the ward where Jake was lying, only to find the curtains drawn. _"Is there something wrong with him"_ came a little voice from outside the drawn curtains.

_"No" came a female from with-in; _"just checking his bandages, I'll only be a few more minutes"_ the female voice replied. Well it seemed like ages to the waiting ladies for the curtains to be pulled back, to reveal their man on the other side only to have their mouths opened wide when the man from behind the curtain was revealed. It wasn't the man that they had come to see someone else had been moved into where Jake once laid. _"Where's the man that was in here last night"_ April blurted out?

"He was transferred to the next ward early this morning" the nurse replied with a smile.

The two excited ladies and walked briskly out of the ward and into the other, where they found their man sitting up laughing at them both. _"What's so funny"_ April said glaring back at him.

"I was just listening to you getting up that poor little nurse next door" Jake chuckled.

"Little my arse"! April said leaning over giving him a kiss. _"You should have seen the size of her"_ as she stood aside to let her mother in to give him a kiss as well.

With that, April was given a tap on the shoulder that scared the shit out of her.

It's Like Living in a dream

"Excuse me dear" comes the same voice that she heard from behind the curtains in the room next door. _"It's the little my arse nurse here, I have to change your boyfriend's dressings"_ reefing the curtains closed in front of April with a chuckle. _"I'll be at least half an hour missy, so I advise you go and get a cup of coffee or find someone else to insult while I change Romeo's dressings"_ the nurse replied with a laugh. April stormed out off with Lexie close behind, with the sound of laughter coming from behind them as they left the room. As they waited for the time to pass, Lexie tried to calm her daughter who was pacing up and down the cafeteria hallway. _"Come and have your coffee the time will pass quicker that way"_ her mother sighed.

Sitting at the table, April stared at the clock watching it slowly tick away. As soon as the half-hour was up, April ran from the table back to the ward only to find the curtains still drawn. _"How much longer will you be nurse"_? April inquired in a nice and pleasant voice hoping, not to offend her again.

"You can see him now missy if you like" the nurse replied.

"Thank you very much" they both said with a smile, as the nurse pulled back the curtains. Giving Jake another kiss, April asked, _"How much longer are they going to keep you in here"_?

"The nurse thinks the doctor might let me go home if I behave myself" Jake replied.

"Well you better behave" Lexie said shaking her finger; _"I can't have you laid up in here all the time up setting the nurses"_ Lexie added smiling.

"When is the doctor going to be to see you"? April asked.

"Right now" comes another voice from behind her scaring the shit out of her as she leaped off the bed.

"I'll have to ask you both to leave so I can examine him first" pointing to the door.

The curtains were be to be closed once more around April's man, which was really pissing April off, for she wasn't able to spend time with her precious Jake. For every time she started to talk to him the curtains were to be closed, she could hardly wait for the doctor to open the curtains again so she could be with her man once more. The curtains opened in a flash and before April could say a word the doctor said; _"are you going to take this man home or do I have to find someone who will"_. Before April could get another word in; _"I'll take him home for you doctor"_ coming from the little my arse nurse. With that, April had all Jake's things in her hand saying to her mother, _"you take these while I help Jake"_; as they hurried him out of the hospital and back to the comfort of the ranch.

Chapter Seven

On their arrival back at the estate, Adam had made up the spare room so the girls could keep an eye on Jake.

"How are you feeling now son" Adam asked.

"OK now that I'm back home Mr Conway" Jake responded.

"Well, I have made up a bed for you in the spare room, so you just go in and lie down, April will show you where it is" Adam insisted.

"Come on Jake" April said taking him by the hand _"I'll show you where you will be sleeping for a while"_.

"No fussing over him April or Jake will never want to leave" Lexie said with a smile.

"Mum"! April blushed leading him by the hand to the room saying, _"take no notice of them"_.

In the room April helped Jake onto the bed, where she fell into his arms as she was laying him down to rest. As their eyes met, April couldn't help giving Jake a big passionate kiss without the prying eyes of her parents. _"Oh Jake! I've been waiting for this moment since you put me on the bus 3 months ago, you have been on my mind all the time"_ embracing him once more. As April left the room, she was to leave Jake with the biggest smile she had ever seen on any man.

Later that night when everyone was asleep, April decided to look in on Jake to see if he was resting comfortably, only to find him sitting up in bed. _"Are you all right"_ April whispered?

"I couldn't sleep" Jake whispered.

"Why, aren't you tired" April asked?

"No not that, I couldn't stop thinking about what you said earlier" he replied. With that remark, April sat on the edge of Jake's bed saying, _"you know my folks will freak if they see us together in here"_.

"I know" Jake replied, _"I could even lose my job and I can't afford to lose it"_ as April drew near. Taking her in his arms where they embraced, not willing to take it any further while April's parents are just up above.

The next morning at breakfast, Lexie asked April if she wouldn't mine looking after Jake while she went into town to do some shopping and to have lunch with Brook. Well, April's eyes lit up like a Christmas tree when she heard the news that she was going to home alone with the man of her dreams. April couldn't get her parents out of the house quick enough, when it was time for them to leave so she could be with her man. As her mother was leaving, she told her daughter not to bother Jake too much for he needed his rest to get better. April waited eagerly for her parent's cars to leave the drive, before heading straight to where the loving arms of Jake lay, undressing as she went.

By the time she reached the side of Jake's bed, she was completely naked. April lent over kissing him softly on the cheek, this caused Jake to roll over on his back where April planted a big kiss on his lips. With that Jake awoke to fine April bending down with nothing on, immediately sitting up whispering; _"what are you doing with nothing on, your folks could walk in at any minute"_.

"Just shut up and get your bloody pants off, they are both in town and won't be home until late" April replied helping him with his boxers. After April finished taking off Jake's boxers, she jumped in bed ready to ride her untamed stallion. Jake softly kissed her lips and caressed her firm little tits with one hand, while the other stroked her cute little arse. April meanwhile ran her finger nails up and down Jake's back, before digging them into Jake's tight butt. Jake shifted the hand that was stroking April's bum and moved it towards her sweet mound of auburn fluff and parted it with his fingers.

The moment Jake's fingers hit her button, April was to let go the grip that she had on his arse and rolled over on her back. Jake then shifted his fingers, only to replace it with his tongue. As his tongue hit her quivering little button, April grabbed Jake by the hair as she arched her back in delight. This was to be the first time any guy had touched her little pussy with their tongue. After a while of munching on April's wet little box, Jake laid beside her letting April take his sticky cock into her mouth. In doing that, she rolled him over on his back, throwing one leg over his shoulder exposing her tunnel of love to his eyes. As they engulfed each other, their orgasms flowed into each other. At that moment, April turned around and perched herself on the enormous dick below. As April rode Jake's cock, Jake gently twisted April's nipples making her ride his cock even faster.

The faster Jake twisted April's nipples the faster April rode his dick and the louder she moaned and sighed with delight. Jake took one hand away from April's tit and inserted his index finger up her arse, making April's eyes roll as his finger rubbed against his immense cock. "Fucking hell" she sighed as she was about to reach another orgasm. That was Jake's cue to roll her over and throw her legs over his shoulders and drive his cock even faster into her twat, making April scream as she reached her second orgasm.

April could tell that Jake was about to reach his second and withdrew his cock from her hot little cunt and placed it up her arse saying; _"fill me up lover"_ as Jake rammed his shaft home. As April was reaching her climax, she dug her finger nails into Jake's back as they reached the peak of their first love session together. Out of breath, the two collapsed in a sweaty heap on the bed. Jake said to April, _"I think we better get cleaned up before your folks come home"_. Grabbing her clothes that were scattered all over the house, April used the shower up stairs while Jake used the down stairs.

Chapter Eight

When Lexie and Adam arrived home they found both Jake and April sound asleep in front of the television, luckily they were in separate chairs. Lexie turned off the television hoping not to wake the young couple, but the moment the television was turned off, the pair immediately woke.

"Back in the land of the living are we" Lexie remarked and then added, _"I hope April didn't bother you too much love"_ looking at Jake.

"No, she only checked on me once this morning" looking over at April.

"How's the eye today son" Adam inquired.

"I'll be OK to work tomorrow sir" Jake replied.

"Are you sure Jake" Lexie replied then adding _"we don't want you over doing it"_.

"No, I'll be fine to work" Jake insisted.

"Are you both up to supper" Lexie inquired?

"Yes" they both replied racing each other to the kitchen.

After supper, they all watched the late night movie before Adam and Lexie retired for bed, leaving the youngsters on their own.

"Now don't keep him up too late darling or we won't get any work out of him tomorrow".

"I won't mother" April replied with a smile. The moment they heard their bedroom door close, they were in each other's arms once more. April put a blanket over their laps just in case one of them came back down stairs. That enabled April to grab Jake's cock and gently masturbate it until it grew to its full length. _"I'll meet you in your room in one hour with no knickers on"_ April whispered into Jake's ear. Then yelled _"good night Jake"_ loud enough for her parents to hear, then turned and kissed his dick on the head before going to her room.

April kept her promise and was in Jake's room right on the dot of an hour. _"What kept you"_ he said with a whispering smile as April was trying to jam her tongue down his throat. Jake lifted her up, making April wrap her legs around his waist. As Jake was already undressed and his dick was as hard as, he was able to slip it into April's hot waiting snatch. _"Oh Jake you are one hell of a lover, you really know how to make a girl feel good"_ bobbing on his cock.

"Why thank you honey, you're not that bad yourself" as he pumped his mammoth cock into his young lover.

April dismounted and bent over the bed letting Jake enter her pussy from behind. While holding onto her thighs, April moaned softly as Jake drove his cock in and out of her sweet little box. Biting her tongue to hold back her excitement as she reached her orgasm!

"Well lover" April said after she was satisfied yet again, _"I told you that I was going to have it when I got home again"_.

"So you did" Jake smiled adding, _"I had a dream that night of making love to you in the pool. That's why I choked on my breaky when you all mentioned about cleaning the pool"_.

"You randy bugger" as she smacked Jake on the dick! _"Well my love; I better go to bed and let you get your strength for tomorrow"_ kissing him on the cheek.

In the morning, Jake was up early and started work before they were even out of bed making up for lost time. When the rest came down for breakfast, Lexie went into Jake's room to fetch him for breakfast for he was the only one not at the table. On entering his room when there was no answer, Lexie found that his bed was made and all his things were gone. _"That ungrateful little bastard"_ Lexie yelled, making April come running to where she laid the night before.

"What's wrong mum"! April asked with a worried look on her face.

"HE'S GONE THAT'S WHAT"! Lexie yelled, adding _"He has taken all of his things and left"_.

"HE CAN'T BE" April yelling back!

"Well look for yourself then" her mother grunted leaving the room. With that April ran out to the house to check his room near the pool, only to find him perched on his mower down at the front of the estate.

When Adam was leaving for the office, he met Jake at the gate. _"Good morning Mr Conway, nice day today isn't it"_ yelling over the noise of the mower.

"Good morning to you to Jake" yelling back as Jake stopped the mower.

"You really gave us a scare this morning, we thought you done a runner like our last handyman" Adam went on to say. _"When Lexie saw all your things were gone, we really went off her tits"_.

Jake bursting out into a fit of laughter, "you're kidding aren't you."

"No I'm not" Adam said as he was about to drive off.

"Well I better go and show them that I'm still here then" laughing his head off, as he started up his mower again and headed of towards the house.

The moment Jake entered the kitchen, he copped an ear full from little April.

"You son of a bitch" April screamed throwing the dish cloth at him hitting him in the face. _"We thought you pissed off like the other mongrel when we couldn't find your things in your room"_ April went on to say.

"Well I thought it was time that I went back to my own room now that I was better" he responded as he threw the dishcloth back at April.

"You could have said something last night before we went to bed" Lexie scolding him from the other side of the table.

"I'm sorry my dears to disappoint you both and besides I didn't think that I would be missed that much" Jake laughed as he headed for the coffeepot.

"If you think you're getting a cup of coffee after what you have just done think again buster" Lexie sneered grabbing the pot.

It's Like Living in a dream

_"Ah come on ladies give a man a break here, I didn't mean any harm" pleading for a cup of coffee. _"Please, Pretty please even may I please have a cup of coffee"_ begging once more.

"All right, but if you ever do that again, I'll kick your arse until it bleeds you hear me" Lexie shaking her fist. After Jake had finished his coffee, he went back to finish mowing the front of the estate.

April asked her Mother if she could go into town to buy a new swim suit and to get her hair cut, while she caught up with friends. _"That'll be fine dear, what time do you think you'll be back"_ Lexie asked her daughter.

"About 5 o'clock, we plan to catch a movie after we get our hair done" April replied.

"OK honey see you when you get back then" as Lexie headed up to her room.

As April was driving down the drive she yelled out, _"hey gorgeous, want anything in town"_?

"No thanks sweetheart" came a reply.

"OK, I'll see you about 5 then" speeding off down the drive just in time to see Jake put his mower in the shed.

Seeing that Jake had finished mowing the lawn Lexie called out to him, _"Jake can you meet me at the pool in 10 minutes please"_. Jake answered by the way of a hand as he walked away from the shed where he had just stored his mower.

"What did you want me for Lexie" Jake asked quizzically?

"Would you mind rubbing some sun screen lotion on my back for me please".

"No, not at all" as Jake fumbled with the cap as Lexie dropped her tiny robe to the deck of the pool, Jake whistled at her fine shape as she laid face down on the deck chair. Lexie just turned her head and smiled as Jake began to rub the lotion into her back.

As Jake reached the middle of her back, Lexie reached around and was about to undo her top only to be stopped by Jake saying _"I'll do that for you Lexie"_.

"Why thank you sweetie" Lexie responded.

As Jake gently massaged the lotion into Lexie's back, she arched her back as she shifted her hair out of the way. This was to give Jake a sneak peak at one of her nice firm tits.

"OK, you can rub a little down the sides please" Lexie said with a sigh.

By this time, Jake had the biggest hard on, as he proceeded to do as he was told. _"A little higher"_ as Lexie arched her back once more. In saying that, Jake had his hands full with Lexie's rock hard breasts. As Jake gently caressed her tits, not only was Jake getting turned but Lexie as well. Lexie let out a little moan, bringing Jake back into reality as he realized what he was doing. Jake quickly took his hands away from Lexie's well-excited tits, making Lexie sit up giving Jake a good look at her very nice set.

"Very sorry Lexie" Jake said with a terrified look only to add, _"No I'm not"_ landing a passionate kiss upon her lips. With that, Lexie's defences were shot. With her tits excitable once more, Jake caressed them as he did only moments before.

Taking Lexie by the hand he lifted her up and carried her to his room, thinking it was only proper to make love to her in the comfort of the bed. Lexie was a little hesitant at first, but with another kiss from Jake she was lifted up and carried into his room. Jake lowered Lexie gently onto the bed taking her bikini briefs with him, while Lexie took of his T-shirt at the same time. Jake knelt beside her spreading her leg exposing her hands off property and slowly moved his head towards her awaiting hole. _"Shit"_ Lexie shrieked, as Jake's tongue found its mark. _"Shit that feels good"_ as Jake worked his magic on her love button. _"Faster, Jake faster"_ Lexie pleaded pushing his head into her snatch.

"Oh yes that's it" as she moaned as her first orgasm was getting near. Lexie started fucking Jake's face as she squealed as she exploded her load.

It's Like Living in a dream

As Jake was making Lexie cum with his tongue, he was undressing himself at the same time. As Lexie reached her orgasm, she reached down lifting Jake's head saying, _"give me your cock"_ making Jake stand up. Lexie grabbed it and took it well into her mouth while she needed his balls, making Jake sigh as Lexie's mouth was like a vacuum cleaner sucking away like there was no tomorrow. Jake's eyes were rolling, as he poured his love juices down her throat. When every last drop was swallowed, Lexie dragged him to the bed where Jake inserted his still rock hard cock into Lexie's eagerly awaiting beaver. As Jake was fucking away, Lexie was to reach her second orgasm, the moment Lexie let loose yet again, Jake was to do also. Jake lowered his sweaty body onto his new lover where they embraced once again.

Chapter Nine

After Lexie had showered, she came out to find Jake packing. _"What the fuck do you think you're doing"_ grabbing his Nap Sack and throwing it to the ground.

"After what has just happened, I figured that I was finished so I was packing".

"Who sacked you, I certainly didn't" Lexie snapped.

"I reckoned from the moment I was playing with your tits, let alone screwing the arse off you I was finished" as Jake went for his Nap Sack once more.

"After what you just gave me! You think I'm going to just let you walk out the bloody door" throwing his nap sack away again and pushing him back onto the bed.

With Lexie still naked and now sitting on Jake's legs, he couldn't help but fondle her beautiful tits once again. Lexie then lowered herself to his mouth so they could be joined as one. At that moment, Jake rolled Lexie over making her let loose of the grip that she had on his mouth. With Jake's cock now rock hard once again he started fucking his new lover once more.

After they had finished making love for the second time, Lexie started to sob.

"What's wrong" Lexie Jake asked as he comforted his older lover.

"This morning when I found all your things missing, I called you some horrible names" as she sobbed on his shoulder. _"I want you to promise me that you won't leave without letting us know first OK"_ Lexie went on to say.

"Shit if I can screw the Boss's wife and still keep my job, who in their right mind would leave". With that Lexie gave him another kiss before lying back onto the bed. Jake was to leave the room and leave Lexie lie there and soak up the memories of what has just happened.

It's Like Living in a dream

Three hours were to pass, before Jake was to re-enter his room to still find Lexie lying there with nothing on. He snuck over and softly caressed her pointed nipples, in doing that, it made Lexie open her legs. It was just enough for Jake to stick his stink finger into her pussy, in doing that Lexie awoke with a start.

_"Time you thought about getting dressed and up to the house before your husband and daughter arrive home" as he stuck his finger into his mouth.

"Why, what time is it" Lexie asked with blurry eyes?

"It is now 4.30" Jake replied pointing to his clock!

On hearing the time, Lexie was out of bed and dressed in no time. Giving Jake a kiss she headed for the door, only to close it again on hearing a car. It was Adam, for he had had a bad day and finished work early. _"Fuck, how am I going to get out of here now without Adam seeing me"_ as she saw her husband slamming his car door.

"You leave it to me, the moment I distract him; you head for the pool OK". With Lexie nodding briskly, Jake left the room.

"Good afternoon Mr Conway how was work today" Jake asked as he waltzed towards Adam.

"Bloody awful, I had to sack two of my best staff members today" Adam replied.

"Why, you catch them robbing your bank" Jake said with a smile as he saw Lexie heading in through the pool gate.

"No I caught them screwing their arses off in the supply room" Adam snuffed as he headed for the house.

"Your home early dear" Lexie said as she came from the pool dripping wet. _"I thought I'd take a dip before I started to prepare supper"_ fuck that was close she mumbled under her breath, as she headed to the house putting her arm around her husband. With that, April pull up looking all pretty and sexy getting a little whistle from Jake as she got out of her car.

"Hi there gorgeous, how was your day" April asked looking at her lover that was just in a pair of shorts and a T-shirt.

"You didn't get up to any mischief in town did you"?

"It was OK I guess, but I would have rather been home here with you" grabbing him by the arse as he went by.

All of a sudden, there was a scream coming from the kitchen. Lexie had cut herself while preparing supper and had passed out by the time Jake and April arrived in the kitchen. Adam came running from the bathroom only in a pair of jocks asking what had happened to his wife.

On seeing the blood, Jake asked where the First-Aid box was. _"I don't think we have one Jake"_ Adam replied looking at April shaking her head agreeing with her father. With that Jake tore his T-shirt to make a bandage to stop the bleeding. When Jake had finished attending to his new lover, he lifted Lexie up and carried her up to her bed. _"Thanks for doing that Jake, I wouldn't have known what to do"_ Adam commented. _"I'll buy a First-Aid kit tomorrow"_ he went on to say.

"The wound will need cleaning before then sir" Jake replied as he ran back down stairs grabbing a set of keys on the bench.

"Wait Jake, I'm coming with you" April yelled running after him.

Upon their arrival at the chemist to buy a well needed First-Aid kit Jake had forgotten his wallet. It was home on his bed, for he had taken it out just before he screwed his young lover's mother and his boss's wife. Turning towards April, _"I don't suppose you have any money on you do you"_ he asked.

"No mine is in my handbag in my car, sorry honey".

Jake turned back around to the young lady behind the counter and explained the urgency for the kit and asked if they could pay for it tomorrow.

"I don't know; I'm only new" the young lass replied.

"Then how do we find out if we can" April asked looking quite mad.

It's Like Living in a dream

"I'll ring the manager, if he says it's OK then I'll let you charge it, be right back".

"Thank you" Jake replied.

The young lady came back and said that they had to leave some sort of identification before the sale can be approved. With that Jake went out to the glove box of the car and produced his license so the credit could be approved. April and Jake thanked the young lady for being so considerate and then left. April drove on the way home and turning towards Jake she asked would her mother be alright? _"Your mum will be fine once I clean the cut to stop it getting infected"_. On hearing that, April turned off the highway and stopped out of sight of the oncoming traffic. Jake asked what she was doing, and then he saw the smile on her face and knew exactly what April had on her mind as he laid his seat back.

April reached over and undone his zipper of his fast tightening jeans to give Jake's growing cock some room. With-in a flash, she had his big dick in her mouth sucking like there was no tomorrow. While April was kept busy, Jake released April's tits from her blouse and was giving them a good working over.

"This is only a sample of what you are going to get tonight" April grinned as she went for his balls. April took his left agate into her mouth and slowly sucked it making Jake's arse rise in sheer pleasure. The moment Jake started to breathe faster, April stopped saying _"that'll do for now"_ doing up her blouse saying; _"we need to get home before dad starts wondering why we are taking so long.

"You little bitch"_ Jake blurted out as he tried to tuck his sizable muscle back into his jeans.

Adam was waiting for the pair to come home as time was getting on and Lexie was in pain from her deeply cut thumb. As they got out of the car, April turned to Jake saying; _"you better do up your zipper before you walk through that door"_.

"Oh shit" as he fumbled with his zip.

40

As they walked through the door Adam asked; _"what took you so long, don't you realise how much pain your mother is in"_ looking at Jake suspiciously adding _"did you have a lot of trouble getting it you were gone for over an hour"_?

_"You have no idea, the amount of bull shit that we had to go through to get it seeing we had no money" April remarked storming off to her mother's bedroom

"Jake, Lexie is asking for you the pain is really bad in her thumb now" pointing to the bedroom.

"I'm on my way" as he sidestepped the suspicious looking father.

While Jake was attending to Lexie, Adam turned to April asking _"April honey"_.

_"Yes daddy" April answered giving her father a cuddle.

"Has Jake ever tried to take advantage of you while you have been home on vacation"?

"No dad, he has been an absolute gentleman to me and hasn't made a single one" giving her father a kiss on the cheek. April smiling to herself, for it wasn't a lie either, for she was doing all the advancing not Jake. _"Why did you ask that for dad"_? April replied looking quite concerned. Before Adam could respond to his daughter's question Jake came down stairs saying; _"Mr Conway, your wife's cut needs a couple of stitches as soon as possible, would you like me to take her to the hospital"_?

"No, you two have your supper; I'll take her to the hospital and thanks for the offer son" patting him on the back then went on to say; _"Jake how come you know so much about dressing wounds by the way"_?

"I was a volunteer at the ambulance station before I came to work for you sir" as he sat down at the table, while April was dishing up supper.

"Oh that explains it all then" as Adam headed up the stairs to fetch his wife.

It's Like Living in a dream

"Dad suspects something is going on between us" April whispered as her father headed off to the bedroom.

"That's great, what did you tell him while I was up attending to your mum"? Jake asked now looking quite concerned.

Just as April was about to answer his question, her parents entered the kitchen where the two young lovers were having their very late supper.

"Keep her hand up above her shoulder Mr Conway, that way it will ease the pain in her thumb" Jake said to Adam.

"Thanks son" as he escorted his wife to the car.

When her parents had left, Jake asked April once again what she said to her father. April's reply was _"he asked if you have made any advances towards me"_.

"How did you answer that one" the stunned handy man asked?

"I told him the truth; I wouldn't lie to my father" April said with a smile as she saw the look on Jake's face change. _"Don't look so worried honey. I told him that you have been nothing but a perfect gentleman and that you haven't made a single move on me. And that's no lie, I have been the one doing all the chasing, now shut up and give me a kiss"_ grabbing him by the arse and drawing him close.

Chapter Ten

On the way to the hospital Adam turned to Lexie saying _"I think there is something going on between April and Jake"_ looking back at the road.

"What gives you that impression dear" Lexie asked as she moaned with pain.

_"Just by the way he looks at her" Adam remarked.

"Remember we were there once ourselves, they are only young and if it happens, it happens, so stop your belly aching and just drive" Lexie snapped at him in a harsh voice.

"Don't you think that she could do better than him" Adam snapping back?

"No I bloody don't, he seem a nice enough boy and I can't see anything wrong with that" yelling at him for the pain was really getting to Lexie now.

"No I suppose you can't, he's probably fucking the arse off you as well while I'm at work" yelling back at her. Not another word was said by either of them as they travelled to and from the hospital.

Back home, Adam was ordered to sleep in the spare room by his cranky wife; and the next morning he left for the office without saying good bye to his family. Lexie waited for the others to come to breakfast so she could ask them if they were sexually involved.

"April your father seems to think that you two are romantically involved, I don't care if you are, just tell me the truth"!

"Yes mum we are" April replied grabbing Jake by the hand.

"How long have you two been lovers"?

"Only a couple of weeks, now I guess, does Mr Conway want me to leave" Jake inquired.

"I don't know, but as I said to you yesterday, I don't want you to leave" Lexie replied.

It's Like Living in a dream

April turned to Jake and then to her mother saying; _"don't tell me that you two are screwing each other"_ letting go of his hand in discuss.

"I'm afraid so love" her mother added.

"Just fucking brilliant! The only man who has ever looked sideways at me and I have to share with my mother. How long have this been going on for, I suppose it's been even since Jake arrived" screaming at her mother and slapping Jake across the face.

No! It only happened yesterday while you were in town and don't blame Jake, I seduced him not the other way round" her mother screaming back at her enraged daughter.

"Both of us in 24 hours, how could you, I've fallen in love with you, you son of a bitch" April screamed as she ran to her room.

_"So have I" Lexie replied running after her with Jake following close behind.

Once all three were in the same room Lexie turned towards Jake saying _"So how are we going to deal with it"_?

"How the hell do I know, I'm in love with the both of you! So where do I go from here" before walking out the door!

Jake went back to his room and packed up his things and was heading for his car, when April yelled to her mother; _"Jake is leaving"_ running out of her room to stop him.

"Like bloody hell he is" running after her!

"I told you that I didn't want you to leave and I meant it" Lexie said throwing his nap-sack on the ground and giving it a kick.

"Well then tell me how we are going to handle this, I love you both" Jake screamed looking at them both.

"I don't know, share you I guess, that's if it's OK with you honey" Looking at her daughter.

"If it is going to be the only way that Jake is going to remain in my life then I'll give it a try to see how it goes; but I have to be his main lover not you mum".

"OK honey, I promise I will give you two as much time together as possible but I also need him as well".

"Now that we have worked this out, let's go and have something to eat all this fighting has really made me hungry" Jake replied as he put his arms around their waist escorting them back to the kitchen.

After they had finished eating Jake went back to his barracks to unpack his clothes once again.

On his arrival back to the kitchen about an hour later both Lexie and April had planned a surprise for their lover. As the unexpected stud waltzed back into the kitchen, he was to two red headed beauties completed naked. _"Bloody hell you two look nice enough to eat"_ he replied rubbing his eyes with shock!

"Well what's stopping you then, don't you think you can handle us both" they said together.

"OK ladies, you are in for the time of your life" dropping his shorts saying _"get your spunky arses up to the bed now."_

Four hours were too pass where the three had the hottest sex session that they ever experienced. After they tidied themselves up, they all sat around thinking of ways that they could keep this romance going. How were they going to keep Adam from finding out, for if he was to find out, they would be all out on their ears.

In the days to follow, the three were never to be seen together, for they agree to keep a low profile whenever Adam was around. Jake even told the girls to treat him like shit, for it was all in aid of convincing Adam that nothing was going no behind his back. Lexie was even more loving to her husband but always thinking of her new lover who was never too far away. April snuck out at night to be with her man that she loved so much and Lexie had her turn during the day while her daughter was out.

It's Like Living in a dream

One day, Brook was to come over for a surprise visit for she had not seen Lexie for a while. Brook was longing to in the arms of her lover once more as well, so as she marched into the lounge room, Brook said to Lexie _"How is it going lover"_. Unknown to Brook, April was lying on the lounge out of sight from Brook, on hearing Brook call her mother lover, she sat up immediately. _"Oh shit_, sorry honey I didn't see April lying there"_. Brook doing her best trying to cover up what she had yelled out.

"Don't tell me you're screwing Mrs Cambridge too mother" looking quite shocked!

"I'm afraid so love" as she gave Brook a kiss on the lips.

"How the hell do you make love without a cock" April asked inquisitively?

"First you can start by calling me Brook not Mrs Cambridge; it makes me sound like an old witch. And if it's OK with your mother we'll show you."

Getting the nod from Lexie, they took April by the hand and led her up stairs to the main bedroom. As the two hot vixens started fondling each other, Lexie turned to her daughter saying; _"if you want you can join in honey"_.

"How gross" April replied peering through her fingers, but the more she watched the more intrigued she became. Unknown of what she was doing, April found herself playing with her own tits. When Brook whispered into Lexie's ear; _"Look, April is playing with herself"_. They stopped what they were doing and went over do April, where her mother undone the zipper on her daughter's dress. Brook knelt down in front of April and slowly lifted up her dress and handed it to Lexie. Brook then kissed April on her sweet little mound that was stilled covered with her lace panties, while her mother took one of her daughter's small but firm tits into her mouth. Brook then proceeded in lowering her little panties exposing her little auburn box saying _"Just like your mother's only younger"_.

With that April stepped out of her fallen knickers as Brook moved her hand up the inside of her leg towards her trembling pussy. This was to make April open wide to let Brook inter her moist little vagina, while her mother continued to suck and nibble on her firm little tit. When Brook got to her feet, they escorted their new young lover over to the king-size bed. This was to be an experience that April was not going to forget in a hurry, as her mother and Brook made a woman out of this young lady.

"Well my dear, now you know how us woman make love without a cock as you put it, what did you think of it"? It took April a little while to come to terms with what had just happened to her beautiful young body before she answered Brook's question.

"Wow! That was something, but I still rather Jake's cock"_ she replied.

"Jake's dick don't tell me little April is screwing your handy man" looking at Lexie.

"Yes, we both are" Lexie said hugging her daughter.

"Shit you have all the luck honey, how long has this been going on" Brook remarked.

"Only a couple of days now" April smiled.

"OK, how the long do you plan to keep this from Adam, you know the man you call your husband".

"For as long as we can" Lexie said staring hard at Brook.

"Why are you looking at me like that for, as if I would tell him something like that! What do you take me for, some kind of bitch".

"No, you are the only one that knows OK" April said with a grin.

"As if you would be going around telling the whole world that you two are screwing your handy man".

The three lovely ladies retired back to the kitchen where they sat around the table with a cup of coffee, when Jake walked in. _"Hello handsome"_ Brook remarked at his nice body.

"Hello yourself sweetheart" as he went to the fridge to grab a can of coke, _"what brings you out this way; don't tell me you came to get laid again"_ as he grabbed it and turned to leave the room. Well when Jake said that, April's mouth opened up in shock.

"You cheeky little shit" Brook replied throwing a biscuit at him as he was leaving the room.

"Does Jake know about you two" April questioned looking quite stunned?

"Yes he saw us in the lounge room the first time we made love" Brook said answering April's question. With that April was now full of questions, as she wanted to know everything by this stage.

"How did it this start, you know, you two".

"Shall I tell her, or you" Brook inquired.

"No I will" Lexie said taking April into the lounge room.

"It all started when your father and I were at a business luncheon about 6 months ago. The luncheon was boring, so your father decided to feel me up under the table. We were both so dam horny; we headed for your father's office".

"OK mum, I don't want to know about your sex life with dad; I want to know how you and Brook got together" April protested.

"If you let your mother finish you'll find out won't you" Brook butted in.

"As I was saying, we headed off to your father's office. We were making love on your father's desk when Brook walked in catching the two of going for it".

"I'll finish it from here" Brook insisted. _"While your father was working up your mother; I was getting turned on as well! I knew where the pair was heading, so I followed them. As your mum was saying, I walked in on them and asked if I could join in"_.

By this time, April was all ears as she followed Brook around the room. _"The pair of us screwed your father for the rest of the afternoon"_ Brook went on to say.

_"The moment we finished, I asked Brook to come over the next day for a cup of tea" Lexie added.

"What happened then"? April butted in saying with her ears well and truly pricked so she didn't miss a single bit. _"I seduced Brook right where you were sitting in the kitchen"_ Lexie went on to say as she gave her daughter a cuddle.

"Does dad know about the tow of you" April asked?

"Shit No! He'll freak out if he knew that his wife was making love to another woman" Lexie reported. The three then went back out into the kitchen where Lexie and Brook fixed lunch, but Brook wasn't interested in anything eat, she to know all about their handy man.

Chapter Eleven

As the time was getting on now, Brook decided it was time to get on home. As she was about to leave, she asked if she could borrow their lover for tomorrow to do some work around her place. Getting the nod from Lexie she turned for the car with mother and daughter following her out. When Brook got into her car she turned to April _"Don't let your mother wear you out dear"_ as she drove away.

"What did Brook mean by that mum"?

"You and me having sex silly", escorting her daughter back into the house letting April's mind wander. Being exhausted after their strenuous love affair, the two red heads retired for a snooze. Jake was unaware, that his three lovers had made mad passionate love without the aid of his dick. Brook was still feeling pretty horny when she left her lady lovers, so she decided to pay Adam a visit at his office.

Knowing full well that Lexie wouldn't walk in on them like she did on them and unsure of the response that she was going to receive from Adam; she was very cautious when she arrived at his office. On her arrival at Adam's office Brook was informed that he was in a meeting and was not to be disturbed.

_"Can you tell me how long Mr Conway will be in his meeting?" Brook asked his Secretary.

"For the rest of the day Mrs Cambridge, I'll let him know that you called".

"Shit" Brook replied as she headed home, to leave her thinking about the day in his office.

Still feeling sexually aroused; Brook headed for her room to make love to her toy dick. Painting a picture of how it was going to be making love to Adam all by herself without having to share him with his wife. After Adam had finished in his meeting, he was informed that Brook had come to see him. Wanting to know what Brook had come to see him for, he gave her a ring. Just as Brook was reaching her orgasm, her phone rang. _"BLOODY

HELL! Who can that be"_ turning off her plastic dick to receive her incoming call.

_*"Hello Brook speaking"_*

_*"Brook its Adam; I believe you call in to see me earlier"_*

_*"That's right, I did"_*

_*"What was it that you wanted to see me about"_*

_*"Nothing important, I was just in the neighbourhood and decided to pay you a visit"_*

_*"I can you come and see you on my way home if that is alright"_*

_*"Only if you want too"_*

_*"OK then, I'll ring Lexie and inform her that I'll be home late, I'll let her know that you wanted to see me and that I will be paying you a visit before I come home"_*

_*"Shit don't tell her that, she'll kill me"_*

_*"OK then, I'll tell her that I'm working late, she'll understand"_* as he hung up the phone.

Adam arrived as planned, to find Brook wearing a see through nighty with no bra or knickers on under her see through nighty.

"You didn't want to talk to me did you" looking at her body in the dim light. Brook said nothing, as she moved towards him putting her arms around his neck and drawing his mouth to hers. Only to be pushed away with Adam saying _"I really don't think I should be here"_

"What isn't my body good enough for you this time"? As her mouth drew closer again!

"No you're my wife's best friend and it doesn't seem right" pushing her away again!

"It didn't bother you in your office, where you screwed me in front of her" Brook protested letting go of her strangle hold on his neck.

It's Like Living in a dream

"That's different she was with us both" Adam protested.

"The only thing different about tonight is Lexie isn't here but I am" as Brook started to undo his belt.

"I can't" grabbing her hands!

"Then fucking piss off I don't need your cock" pushing him out the door.

With Lexie and Brook being close friends, Brook rang and told her that she tried to seduce Adam just now hoping that she would understand. The shocked Brook was bewildered when Lexie said that it didn't matter to her if she screwed the son of a bitch.

**"But I took advantage of your trust"** **Brook sobbed**

**"I know that lying bastard is playing around on me, why do you think I started fucking the arse of my handy man for"**

**"So you don't mind me trying to get Adam into bed then"****?**

**"No you can fuck the son of a bitch as much as you like, that's if you can that is for I can't get much out of him"** hanging up the phone as he walked in the door.

"Who was that on the phone honey" Adam asked as he put his briefcase down.

"No one important" leaning across to give him a kiss on the cheek. _"Is that a new after shave you're wearing"_ giving him a sniff.

"No why?" Adam questioned his wife's sniff.

"Because it smells like perfume too me, you two timing bastard" slapping him across the face. _"You're in the bloody dog house again and believe me, I'll find out who you're screwing if it's the last thing I do"_ running to her room.

April heard the argument her parents were having and went to her mother's aid after she heard her crying in her room.

"What was all that about mum"?

"Your rotten father has been with another woman".

"So, your fucking someone else as well, don't you think that's fair" she whispered.

"But he has been doing it for years; I have only just done it". With that April cuddled up to her mother on the bed and softly started stroking her hair.

"You're a wonderful daughter" kissing her on the lips. Before they knew it, they were going at it full on. April lowered the hand that was stroking her mother's hair and placed it on her mother's knickers.

As Lexie caressed her daughter's breasts, April slipped her fingers under her mother's panties and into her mother's waiting vagina. April's fingers moved around until they found Lexie's clitoris and with her thumb and index finger now wrapped around it. April gently massaged it, making her mother squirm with delight. With their bodies getting all hot and excited, they undressed each other and resumed their love making in an oral position in the middle of the king size bed.

While Lexie and April were in this position, Lexie shifted her tongue towards her daughter's arse hole making April do the same. As mother and daughter were enjoying each other's company, while Adam was licking his wounds in the spare room down stairs.

The next day Jake went over to Brook's as arranged thinking that he was going to get laid by his third lover, but found a list of jobs that Brook wanted done instead. Grabbing the note in discuss, he proceeded to attend to this mammoth list of little jobs that Brook had lined up for him. As he worked his arse off, he didn't see Brook standing in front of her window watching. It was the hardest day's work that he had put in since he was employed. Brook had worked him so hard, that he developed blisters on both of his hands. For Brook was still in a shit from being rejected from Adam last night that she took it out on poor Jake.

At the end of the day, Jake was that knackered, that he didn't even come up to the house for super. He just had a shower and went straight to bed. In the morning Jake could hardly move a muscle in his body, for it ached from tip to toe, from the hard day that he put in yesterday. With Adam not being able to speak to Lexie for a couple of days because he was out of town, the moment he arrived home he tried to explain where he was the other night.

As he started to explain, he was cut short with Lexie saying, _"I know where you were the other night. Brook rang me right after she booted you out the door"_.

"Then you know that nothing happened between us, so why are you being such a bitch for then".

"Because I know that you're playing around on me".

"I haven't been with anyone but you and Brook in my office, which you encouraged, remember".

"I'm not talking about that time in your office I know about that, it's all the other ones I'm talking about"_.

"I haven't been with anyone else I swear".

"I still don't believe you".

"It's the truth" pleading for her to except his word.

"I still don't believe you, that's why April and I are going to my mother's for the rest of the holidays" as Lexie headed for the toilet locking the door behind her. Adam tried to convince his wife that he hadn't been cheating of her while standing outside the toilet door.

"You still here, I thought you'd be gone by now" yelling from inside.

_"Have it your way" as he punched the toilet door as he left, scaring the living shit out of her.

Adam stormed out of the house, only to run into Jake waltzing up to the house.

"Good morning Mr Conway, nice day isn't it" Jake said with a smile.

"What's so fucking great about it" he grunted. _"and I'm not paying you just to walk around playing with your dick, now get to work"_ he added.

Poor Jake thought he was hit by a bus as he turned around heading for the work shed. _"Boy he's in a big shit today; he must have got a knock back again last night"_ Lexie told Jake that she and April were going to visit her mother's for the rest of the holidays and to do as Adam asked.

_"You pair think you can go that long without me" smiling back at her.

"Well we will just have too" giving her handy man an even bigger smile back.

Later that day at work, Adam thought up as many odd jobs as he could. He even ordered for a shipment of paint to be delivered to the estate for he wanted to keep Jake as busy as possible. It was his way of getting some kind of revenge.

When Adam came home, Jake told him about the shipment of paint that was delivered here by mistake.

"It's no mistake, I want the whole place re-painted, both inside and out by the time the girls get back. And in between the painting you can get stuck into this little list as well"!

"Holy shit he's really got the rags on today" mumbling to himself as he proceeded to look at the long list of odd jobs.

In the morning, Jake started cleaning the outside of the house to get it ready for painting when Adam came out. _"I see you have started already, that's good"_ as he headed off to the office. With Jake's hands aching with every movement caused by his blisters he received from Brook's, he was glad when it was time to knock off for the day, only to face it all again the next morning.

With the days growing longer and the pain in his hands getting worse, Jake decided to stop cleaning and take a break on the mower. That night, Jake soaked his poor battered up hands in some warm salt and vinegar water to help with the recovery of his blistered hands. As the days went on, Adam eased up on his handy man and gave him a couple of days off to re-gather his strength.

It's Like Living in a dream

With the tension how easing between them Adam and Jake talked over a couple of beers. Adam apologized for the way that he had treated Jake over the past week; he even took time off to help Jake paint the house. After the outside was painted, Adam turned to Jake and shook his hand for a job well done. _"Let's piss these paintbrushes off and go fishing for a couple of days"_.

"You've won me" Jake replied throwing his brush over his shoulder.

"We'll leave tomorrow about 5 in the morning that's if you're awake that is" patting him on the back.

"I'll have the car ready and waiting before you even have time to have a piss" Jake laughed.

The next morning Jake had the car packed and was tooting on the horn yelling _"Are you ready yet, it's time to go"_

"I haven't had time to even have a piss yet" yelling back as he burst into a fit of laughter.

"I told you I would be ready before you had time for a piss" laughing with him.

"So you did, so you did".

"OK Mr Conway where are we going" Jake asked as Adam reached the car?

"First of all, you can start by calling me Adam, this Mr stuff is giving me the shits and making me feel old".

"OK Mr Conway, only joking Adam" Jake chuckled.

"We are going to a spot where the brim are as sweet as nectar and not a sole to be seem" Adam replied.

"Then what the heck are we doing standing around here for, this spot sounds like heaven" pushing Adam into the car.

In the next two days, Jake and Adam became good pals, laughing and telling stories while they drank heaps of booze. All of a sudden and out of nowhere

Adam asked, _"How's come I haven't seen you with a girlfriend yet? God knows you certainly have the body to catch them"_. Adam went on to say.

Upon hearing Adam's comments, Jake choked on his beer as it went down the wrong way.

"You OK mate" slapping Jake on the back; getting a nod from Jake as a sign of yes. _"Well about your love life, who are you laying these days"_ Adam asking again. Jake had to think fast before Adam puts two and two together saying, _"How do you think I got all these blisters"_? With that Adam choked on his beer as he tried to drink and laugh at the same time.

Coughing and spitting Adam recovered saying; _"Who are you really fucking Jake"_?

"No at the present moment", which wasn't a lie; because Lexie and April had gone away for a holiday. _"But I do fancy Brook Cambridge though"_ Jake went on to say, causing Adam to chock once again.

"You better give this shit away" Jake laughed as he slapped Adam on the back.

"Brook"! Adam remarked after catching his breath, _"Isn't she a bit old for you Jake"_?

"No I don't think so, but you must admit, she still has a great body though".

"That she does, that she does" as he remembered her standing there in the dim light the night she tried to seduce him.

"You know I went to see her the other week" Adam confessed.

"You're joking" Jake remarked.

"No she was standing there in a see through nighty, no bra, no knickers on for that matter. Shit she looked gorgeous standing there with nothing on. Her nice firm tits just waiting to be sucked and her blonde pussy just waiting for a nice hard cock to be shoved in it".

"Did you fuck her" Jake asked in a soft toned voice.

It's Like Living in a dream

"I swear on my mother's grave I didn't fuck her, but I could have, God knows my dick wanted too".

"What did you do then" Jake asked as he took another sip of his beer?

"I stopped her, as she was about to undo my belt, which pissed her off something chronic" as he put his empty tinnie with all the others.

"Then what happened" finishing off his while handing Adam another?

"Brook asked me to leave" cracking the top off his new beer, _"I left and went home to Lexie, end of story"_.

"Fuck I would have screwed the arse off her if I had the chance" Jake barked as he too cracked the top off his beer.

The moment Jake took the top off his beer; his line was to go for a spin. _"Don't just sit there; grab the bloody thing"_ Adam shouted. As Jake was about to pull in the biggest brim that he and Adam were to see, Adam's line also went for a tumble.

"You're on your own mate" just grabbing it just before it went into the river.

"You little beauty"! Jake yelled as he landed his fish. _"You want a hand with yours"_?

"Piss off I've been pulling these in while you were just a twinkle in your daddy's eye" Adam boasted!

The moment Adam said that, his line broke sending him backwards into the fire. Jake fell to the ground laughing his guts out as he saw Adam diving into the water to put out the fire that was burning his arse. That was to be the end of their fishing trip, for Jake had to rush Adam to hospital for burns to his pride and joy. That meant that he had to finish the rest of the painting by himself and that meant more dam blisters he yelled as drove back home.

Chapter Twelve

Jake was Just about finished painting the last room, when to girls came back from their holiday. April yelled out, _"Where are you Jake"_ as he wasn't anywhere to be seen.

"I'm up in your room painting" he screamed back. April ran up to meet him at the top of the stairs, _"Boy I have missed you"_ laying a big wet one on him. _"And I've missed you as well"_ as he came up for air.

"And what about me, did you miss me as much" Lexie said? hitting him with a double question as she took her turn on his lips.

"Just as much as April", coming up for air once again.

"Whose idea was it to paint the whole house" Lexie asked?

"Adam's, he really got the shits right after you two left and he's had me working my arse off ever since" Jake remarked.

"Where is the son of a bitch anyway, I suppose he's out screwing some bimbo" Lexie bitched.

"Now don't get all worried when I tell you where he is OK" as Jake started to chuckle before breaking into a fit of laughter, stopping long enough to add; _"He is lying flat on his belly in hospital"_ before breaking back into another fit of laughter.

"What did some jealous husband stab him in the arse" Lexie replied.

"No, not quite" as he was started to laugh his head off again.

"Then what happened to dad then" April said with a worried look on her face.

"You promise not to laugh when I tell you both" laughing again.

"We promise" they both said together.

"Well come down stairs and I'll make you both a cup of coffee as I tell you" said their laughing painter.

It's Like Living in a dream

"Come on; Tell us, we're dying to know what happened" April replied smacking him on the arse.

"Well, Adam was feeling sorry about the way he was treating me after you both left and decided to take me fishing. We were sitting around the camp fire talking and drinking beer, when I caught a fish. Adam was helping me bring it in, man it was a beauty, and I'll show you it" heading for the freezer.

"Just tell us what happened" Lexie snapped.

"Don't you want to see my fish" lifting up the lid of the deep freezer.

"No I don't want to see your dumb fish; I want to know what happened to my father" April said stamping her feet.

"OK then, now where was I" he asked.

"You had just caught that dumb fish" stamping her feet again.

"That's right, I just about to land this beauty" lifting the lid again.

"Forget about that fucking fish" April said punching him in the arm spilling his coffee.

"Now look what you done" heading for the sink to get a cloth.

"Just tell us what happened, or I'll punch you again" as she closed her fist.

"OK, OK now where I was again" he said copping another punch. _"I know I was just about to land this beauty when your dad's line went as well, _"you sure you don't want to see my fish"_?

"No we bloody don't"_ they both screamed.

_"OK as I was saying, Adam's line went and he left me to land it myself. After I landed mine, I asked if he wanted a hand to land his. Now quoting his own words, _***I've been landing these bastards before you were even a twinkle in your daddy's eye*** when his line broke sending him into our camp fire setting his arse on fire!

When Jake finely told them what had happened to their love one, the two girls laughed their pretty little heads off. They laughed that much that tears were rolling down their cheeks. _"You promised you wouldn't laugh"_ as the tears fell down from his eyes as well.

"We can't help it" they said catching their breath, before starting again.

"How is his bum anyway" Lexie inquired as she gathered herself?

"Full of blisters last time I saw" Jake laughed causing them to laugh along with him once more.

_"Well he won't bother us for a while then" Lexie remarked putting her cup in the sink, only to laugh out loud once again.

"April you will have to sleep in the spare room tonight, I haven't finished painting your room yet" as Jake headed back to his room still laughing his head off.

_"OK"_ she replied; _"We'll see you in the morning then"_.

With sheer exhaustion from a hard day on the paintbrushes, Jake didn't take much rocking to sleep before he was out like a light. The girls on the other hand were awake must of the night by the smell of the freshly painted house. In the morning, Jake went up to the house nice and refreshed only to fine the girls asleep at the table holding on to a cold cup of coffee. _"Hard night ladies"_ waking them up as he entered the kitchen.

_"We were up most of the night from the smell of the paint" April mumbled closing her eyes again.

"Go down to my room, there's no paint fumes in there" Jake added; with that the girls stumbled their way down into bed and weren't seen for most of the day, leaving Jake to finish off the rest of the painting. When they finally surfaced late in the afternoon Jake remarked _"It's about time you two woke up I was starting to think you were both dead"_.

_"Ha! Ha!"_ April replied heading for the fridge saying, _"What's in here to eat, I'm starving. Jake had cooked his fish and had left it in full sight of April's peering eyes.

It's Like Living in a dream

"Holy shit mum! Take a look of the size of this fish here. Is this the one that you caught Jake" taking it out to show her mother.

"That's her" Jake smiled.

"She's a beauty all right Jake" Lexie said as she admired the freshly cooked fish.

"Well let's eat her" getting down some plates.

"When did you cook it" Lexie asked.

"Not long before you two surfaced" as he started to dish it up.

"This is beautiful" April said as she shovelled more into her mouth, getting the same response from her mother.

"Well, I'll leave you two to clean up in here while I go and clean up those bloody paintbrushes" as he took another piece and headed out the door.

Just short of the door Jake stopped and turned his head towards the girls saying, _"gee it is great to have you both back home I have missed you pair"_.

"Well my sweet we have missed you as well haven't we mum" April said with a lustful smile.

"You're not wrong there April my love" replying with the same lustful smile letting him continue on his way.

Chapter Thirteen

As night fell upon the freshly painted house, Jake had just finished cleaning up the paintbrushes and put the rest of the paint in the shed as April sang out _"we're sleeping in your room tonight, you can have the spare bed room"_.

"Pig's arse I am, if you're sleeping in my bed you'll be sharing it with me" yelling back at her.

"That's what I told mum you might say" running down to him.

"If you two are sleeping with me, then I'm in the middle" as he put his arm around her waist heading for the shower.

"Shit you stink of turps" pushing him aside.

"That is why I am going for a shower" dragging her back to his side.

As soon as Jake entered his room, he stripped off right in front of April's bulging eyes.

"The look in your eyes, anyone would think you haven't seen a dick before" as he was about to headed for the shower.

"Not for some time" she added.

"Leave it alone" slapping her hand as she went for his saggy dick. _"There will be time for that after I get rid of this turps perfume that you reckon I'm wearing"_ taking off to the shower.

Jake knew that April would not be far behind him as he closed the door. But unknown to April, Jake had locked it so she couldn't enter while he was in the shower.

"Where is lover boy" her mother asked as she entered the room to find her daughter lying on Jake's bed with nothing on.

"The shit went for a shower and locked the bloody door so I couldn't get in" April remarked, getting a little chuckle from her mother.

It's Like Living in a dream

"It's not funny" thumping the pillow. Jake knew that April was pissed off with him for locking the door, so he took his time in the shower. Jake was in there for over an hour before he decided to come out only to fine both April and Lexie lying on his bed with nothing on.

"You two look like you're after something" as he approached the bed.

"That was a low down trick that you just pulled" April said as she took him by the arm lowering him to the bed.

"I didn't want to spoil it, so I made you wait".

"More like suffer" April protested.

"We have plenty of time" Jake responded.

"Yes all night long" Lexie said as her hands started to go down on their man, followed by her daughter. April took Jake's large cock into her mouth, while her mother took one of his balls into hers.

Well into the late part of the morning, the threesome groped, fondled, caressed and screwed each other before retiring to gather their energy to face another day. As Jake closed his eyes, he believed that he was the luckiest man on the face of the earth as the loves of his life lay lying in his arms. When morning broke, Lexie awoke and went up to the house to fix breakfast, leaving the others to have some time together. Not long after her mother left, April awoke with a fully charged battery and started working on her lover while he was asleep.

When Jake awoke, he found April hanging off the end of his slowly rising dick. _"Didn't you have enough of that last night"_ peering through his tried eyes?

"That was last night, this is today" unleashing it, only to re-engage her lips where she had them the night before. When they had finished what April had started, they walked up to the house arm in arm to join Lexie in the kitchen.

"I suppose we better go and see your father after breakfast, do you want to come with us Jake" Lexie asked?

"No thanks I better stay here because I'll only piss myself laughing at him and he might sack me"_ smiling back at her. _"Besides, I still have a lot of work to do before Adam gets out of hospital. I don't want him to come home thinking that I've been screwing his wife while he is lying in a hospital bed now do I"_ smiling back at her.

"And what about his daughter" April was quick to add?

"It wouldn't look all that bad if he found out that I was screwing you honey half as much as it would be if he found out about your mother and I would it" Jake was quick to respond.

"When you put it that way, I totally agree with you baby" as she gave him a kiss on the cheek as she started to eat her breakfast.

The moment the two girls arrived at the hospital, they went up to the front desk to inquire what ward Adam was in. _"We are here to see Mr Adam Conway; he was admitted the other day with a burnt bum"_ Lexie giggled. Not thinking it was funny, the nurse said with a stern voice; _"you'll find Mr Conway in ward 6, bed number 4 on the 3rd floor. Turn left as you get out of the elevator and you will find him half way down the corridor"_ pointing to the elevators.

"Snotty nose little tart" Lexie said to her daughter as they entered the elevator. Holding back their laughter, as they entered the ward where their blustery laid Lexie asked _"how is your poor little bum darling"_ as they both started to laugh.

"It's not funny" Adam snapped.

"That must have been some fart dad to cause that many blisters" making the whole ward burst out laughing.

"If you two have just come here to make fun of me, then you can jolly well piss off" causing a hush of silence throughout the ward.

"What can't you take a little joke honey" as she gave her husband a kiss on the back of the head.

"I'm sorry daddy for what I said" April added as she gave her father a kiss on the cheek.

"From what Jake said that must have been some fish to make you fall back that far" Lexie giggled.

-"It was bigger than that tiny thing that Jake caught"_ Adam remarked.

"How do you know that, did you see it" April asked?

"Well not exactly, but if I could have landed the dam thing I could have proven it" Adam stated.

"We've seen the size of Jake's" April replied pointing down at her crutch at her mother, out of sight of her father eyes.

"Mine would have been bigger than Jake's little tiny sardine" Adam snapped.

_"No Jake's is bigger than yours honey" looking April as she smiled looking down at her crutch as well.

-"It would so have been"- Adam protested.

"Not did your poor little bum get burnt; I think your ego copped it as well" Lexie remarked.

_"What are you talking about"- Adam grunted.

"I'm saying that you're jealous that Jake caught a fish and you didn't" Lexie remarked doing her best to disguise her comments and the size of Jake's cocks and the size of her husband's.

"All right, but when I get out of here I'll show that little shit who is the better fisherman" as he clinched his fist.

"Oh well April love, I think it's time we left" bending down to give her husband a half-hearted kiss on the lips.

"OK mum" April replied walking around to give her father another kiss.

"I want to see Brook on our way home from the hospital if you don't mind" getting a nod of approval from her daughter.

Chapter Fourteen

Brook was just about out her driveway, when Lexie and April met her at the gate.

"I was just on my over to see you two" Brook yelled out.

"Well we'll meet you back up at the house then" Lexie said as she drove on through. Brook done a U-turn and followed them up to the house pulling up alongside as they stopped.

"How was your holiday love" giving April a kiss on the cheek.

"It was good to see grandma again, but I was glad to get back home though".

"And how was yours honey" giving Lexie a kiss as well?

"About the same as April's I guess".

"Well come on in and tell me all the gossip, while I put the kettle on".

_"Have you heard what happened to daddy" April asked with a smile?

"No please do tell, I am all ears" as Brook's ears pricked up.

"You tell Brook mother".

Just as Lexie was getting to the interesting part, the kettle started to boil.

"Hold it right there until I make the tea, I don't want to miss a single bit of this" as Brook quickly made a pot of tea while Lexie got down the cups.

"OK please do go on this sounds interesting" as Brook sat down.

When Lexie reached the part about the fire, the three of them were now in a fit of laughter, laughing fit to kill.

"Wait there's more" as Lexie went on to finish her story. This was to make all their tits ache with laughter, as Lexie finished telling Brook what had happened.

It's Like Living in a dream

"How is the poor bastard now?" Brook inquired as she composed herself long enough to ask, before breaking out in another fit of laughter.

"Lying in a hospital bed with his arse in the air in a lot of pain" April laughed.

"Well I'll go and see him tomorrow then" Brook smiled.

After they had finished telling Brook all the gossip and their tea, Lexie turned to April.

"Well April dear, it's time we went home to see what our man is doing".

"OK mum" as she gave Brook good bye kiss on the lips.

"See you later sweetie" as she returned her kiss. _"You take care of her"_ as she turned and gave Lexie a passionate kiss.

"I will" Lexie replied.

As they were walking out the door, Brook asked if she could borrow Jake for the day. _"The grass seems to grow over night here"_ she went on to say.

"I can't see anything wrong with that, do you honey" turning to her daughter.

"You can use him on only one condition Brook" April replied.

"And what would that be honey"?

"That you promise not to work him as hard as you did last time" giving Brook a cuddle.

"I promise" kissing young April on top of the head.

When they arrived home, they found Jake weeding the garden. Lexie leaned out the car window saying; _"You'll be working over at Brook's tomorrow Jake"_.

"That's great" he replied as he looked down at his freshly healed hands as they drove away. _"Fuck! I just got over the last bloody episode of her dam place he"_ said to himself out loud. _"But they're the boss and I said that I could do both places"_, as mumbled away to himself as he weeded away.

In the morning, Jake went over to Brook's place as arranged and started looking for the dreaded note of things to do. When he couldn't fine the note he knocked on the door yelling out _"you home Brook"_!

"I'm up stairs; I'll be down in a minute. Come on in and make yourself a cup of coffee, I'll be down shortly" yelling back at him.

"Do you want one as well"?

"That'll be lovely thanks honey".

After Jake had made the coffee he looked up to the ceiling yelling _"coffee's ready"_.

"There's no need to shout I'm just here" freighting the crap out of him, making him spill hot coffee all over his hands and down the front of his clothes.

"Holy shit! look what you made me do" as he went to the sink to run cold water over his burning hands.

"Are you all right" Brook inquired looking quite concerned.

"Yes I think so" as he turned to acknowledge Brook's concern.

When Jake turned around and saw what Brook was wearing, he soon forgot about his burning hands. _"What are you wearing; or should I say what you are almost wearing"_?

For Brook was wearing the same nighty that she wore the night Adam came over to visit. She was wearing it in the same manner that she wore it when Adam was there, on knickers or bra.

"Do you like it"?

"Yes! Very much so" as he let her put her arms around his neck giving her a big passionate kiss.

It's Like Living in a dream

"Shit they hurt" as he remembered his hands, turning back to the sink for more water.

"Let's get you out of those wet clothes" taking off his shirt before undoing the belt that was holding up his shorts. The moment Brook grabbed his belt; Jake could feel his dick starting to rise. As Jake's shorts dropped to the floor, Brook followed them and kissed him on the cheek of his arse. In doing that, Jake turned around letting Brook lower his jocks to the floor as well. With his dick now free to rise to its fullest; it made Brook's eyes light up with delight.

"How about we put those wet clothes in the wash and adjourn to my bed". Before Jake had time to reply, Brook had his cock into her mouth giving it a good hard sucking. She then gathered up his wet clothes and took them and put them in the washing machine, before taking Jake up to her waiting bed.

While Brook and Jake were going hard at it; Lexie and April were to arrive and went up to Brook's room where all the noise was coming from. When they opened up the door and saw the two; April bellowed out _"What do you think you're doing with our lover"_!

"I would like to know the same" Lexie shouted!

"Let me explain" Jake said.

"Know I will" Brook said getting off the bed.

"Don't bother trying to explain" Lexie said pushing her back onto the bed.

"Let us try to explain" Jake protested.

"We don't want to hear your explanations" as April gave him a slap across the face.

"Get you clothes and get on home we'll talk there" pointing to the door. Jake didn't say another word, as he walked past the two angry ladies and headed for the laundry to retrieve his wet clothes. The two were to have a big argument with Brook before they left. Lexie told Brook that their friendship was now over, before leaving to have it out with Jake when they got home. Jake was in his room changing, when the two hot headed ladies arrived home.

"How long have you been screwing the arse off Brook for"? April screamed as she barged into his room.

"That is none of your business" as he tried to leave the room, only to be pushed back by Lexie.

_"And where do you think you're going?" she asked.

"Out to do some work, that is what you're paying me to do isn't it".

"I don't think so" shoving him onto the bed; _"you're going to finish what you started over at that bitch's place isn't he April"_ making him undress.

"Yes why should she get all the glory of our man".

Meanwhile back at the hospital, the doctor was about to release Adam.

"I think you're ready to go home today Mr Conway"_.

"About time, this place was starting to get to me" as he went for his clothes.

"Do you have a ride home Mr Conway"?

"Yes I have my car down stairs in the lock up" Adam replied.

"Very well, I'll leave you to get changed then" as the curtains were pulled back around.

Adam couldn't get out of hospital quick enough, when the doctor gave him the OK to leave. Adam tried to call Lexie at the estate, to let her know that he was on his way home. When there was no answer form either his wife or his daughter at the estate, _"I'll just have to surprise them both when I get home"_ he said as he hung up the phone.

It's Like Living in a dream

With his arse still a little tender from his fishing trip, Adam had to stop a few times and get out and walk around to give his poor little bum a rest from the seat.

Meanwhile back at the estate, his wife and daughter were deeply involved in a three way love affair with his gardener. The three of them didn't hear Adam's car as he drove up the drive, for Jake had his music turned up and they were not able to hear anything. When Adam didn't fine either his wife or his daughter in the house, he headed down to ask Jake if he knew where they were because their cars were still in the drive. As Adam to walk in on the threesome he was to catch his gardener choking his wife, while she was licking out his daughter.

"What the fucking hell is going on here" as he walked in catching them red handed.

You could have heard a pin drop as Adam throw Jake's tape recorder to the floor.

_"You pair of fucking sluts" Adam yelled as he gave his wife a back hand across her face.

Jake came to Lexie's aid, only to receive a punch in the mouth from Adam, which sent him back onto the bed.

"I want you out of right now and if you think you're getting what is owing to you, forget. Now start packing, I want you out of here by the time I get to the house or I'll blow you fucking ball off, now get." _"As for you two, get your fucking arses up to the house, I'm not finished with either of you"_ turning around giving Jake another smack in the mouth as he got up off his bed.

Following his wife and daughter up to the house, Adam was to give April a good kick in the arse sending her to her room while he took it out on Lexie. April watched from her window as Jake took off in a cloud of dust, realizing just how much she was in love with Jake, she ran after him.

"And where do you think you're going" yelling at his daughter to get back to her room.

"I'm not a fucking child any more, I love Jake and I'm going after him" she screamed running out the door.

"Wait! April, I'm coming with you" breaking free of Adam's grip.

"You two go out that door, don't think you're coming back" as he tried to stop Lexie from leaving.

"Get out of my way" Lexie said as she kicked her husband in the balls, _"he's a far better lover than you will ever be"_ running after her daughter.

_"Where do you think he would go mum?" as they drove off after their man.

_"We'll try Brook's place first; he might have gone there."

Brook was surprised to see them after the big fight that they had earlier in the day.

"I'm really sorry for what happened this morning, it wasn't intended, it just happened" not letting them really know that she had full intentions of getting screwed by their lover.

"It's all right, Jake told us what happened and if that happened to us we both would have done the same thing" as they both gave Brook a big hug.

"So what brings you two back over here"?

"We are looking for Jake; we were hoping that he came over here after daddy kicked him off the estate" April said as she started looking around calling his name.

"He isn't here honey and why are you two so upset for"?

_"The son of a bitch was allowed to come home and he caught us both in bed with Jake" Lexie explained.

"Please tell me your joking and that your bullshitting me".

"No my arse still hurts from his foot" April said giving it another rub.

It's Like Living in a dream

"No, he didn't come back here". _"What makes you think he would come here for after you caught him in bed with me, I would be the last place he would go I think"_.

_"Well we'll try the _'Lion's Den'_; they might know where he is"_ Lexie said as they all ran for the car.

Speeding off in search of their man, they headed for the Den, only to be told that they had just missed him by 1 hour.

"Did he say where he was going" April asked?

"Well he said that he was going to sell his car, then head up north" the bar tender replied.

"Thank you" they all said as they ran out the door to check all the used car lots for Jake's car.

Three hours later, April spotted it at the side of one of the buildings.

"There it is mum" as Lexie jammed on the breaks. Exiting the car as fast as they could they ran inside where Brook asked; _"the owner of that car outside your building, did he say where he was going"_?

"Why, is the car stolen" the bewildered sales man asked?

"No, nothing like that" Lexie replied, _"We just like to know where he is that's all"_.

"He told me that he was catching the 1.30pm bus for the north, why what did he do".

"Thanks" as they all ran for the car once again leaving the salesman with a puzzled and concerned look on his face.

"What time is it now" April asked?

"It's 4pm all ready" Brook said as she looked at her watch.

"That means he has two and a half-hours head start on us all ready" April said as she started to sob.

"We'll find him love" her mother said softly.

"We better I love him so much" as she cuddled into Brook.

"We all do" Brook said kissing her on the head.

"Have you fallen for him too" Lexie remarked.

"I'm afraid so, how can you not fall in love with that man now get driving before we all lose him".

The three lovely ladies headed off in search of the man that has made them all so very happy. The only man that has treated them all so very perfect. The man, which neither of them can now live without.

They found out which bus he caught and that it had left two hours ago, so they set off knowing it was going to be a long chase. They headed for the nearest service station to fuel up and to gather some supplies for the long trip ahead. At each bus stop they checked to see how far the bus was ahead of them and to change the driver, as each took their turn at the wheel. With the miles getting longer and the distance between them and the bus getting shorter, they were racing against the clock all the way.

With the rocking of the car putting April to sleep, Brook turned to Lexie saying; _"why don't you get some sleep shut eye as well. We all need to be alert if we are going to catch this bloody bus"_.

_"Yes I guess you're right, wake me when it's my turn to drive" as she closed her eyes and cuddled up to her daughter. As Lexie cuddled up to April, April woke up saying _"Is it my turn all ready"_?

"No, just go back to sleep, I'll wake you when it is honey" Brook said looking at her in the rear-view-mirror.

At the next station, Brook pulled in for more fuel; this was to wake up both mother and daughter.

"I'll fuel this heap up while you two check on that dam elusive bus".

_"OK"_ Lexie said as she rubbed her eyes.

Before Brook had time to finish fuelling up the car, Lexie and April came running out saying _"the bus had not long left, have you finished filling up the car yet"_? With that, Brook hung up the pump and raced inside to pay the attendant; throwing $100 dollars on the counter saying _"keep the change"_. Lexie had the car running and was waiting outside the door ready for Brook to jump in.

Before Brook had a chance to buckle up, Lexie had the tyres smoking as she drove off after the bus.

"How far away is the bus now" Brook asked?

"Only 20 minutes up the road and he is still on it" April said all excited.

"Well put your foot down" Brook said getting all excited like April as they entered onto the highway once again.

It was to take then almost an hour before they saw the tail lights of what could be the long sought after bus they were looking for and Lexie had the car going as fast as she dared.

When Lexie was in sight of the bus, she started flashing her lights to attract the driver's attention, but the driver was taking no notice and would not acknowledge her signal. So Lexie came alongside the driver, where both Brook and April leant out the window pointing to the wheels on his bus.

"Look at this crazy bitch" the driver yelled out.

With Brook and April still pointing at the wheels of the bus the bus driver finally realised where they were pointing and had no hesitations in pulling over to see what was wrong with his bus. The moment the big bus came to a halt, the driver started to ascend from with-in only to be bomb barred by three very excited and weary ladies who had come looking for their lover.

"What is going on here" the stunned bus driver said as he was trampled to the floor.

"We are after one of your passengers" the ladies said as they looked for their long sort after lover.

"What are you all doing all this far north" Jake said looking quite shocked?

"We have come to take you back home to my place" Brook said looking at the others.

"Well we can't go back to mine, Adam said that he was going to blow his balls off if he caught him anywhere near the place" Lexie said.

As April started to escort Jake off the bus and into the awaiting car outside, they were comforted by a very angry bus driver saying _"I don't think so ladies"_.

_"It's all right sir" Jake said; _"they meant you know harm"_.

"So you're willing to go with them then".

"Yes" as he put his arms around April and Lexie.

"Are you sure mate, there are not forcing you to get off are they"?

"No I'm willing to go" Jake smiled as he gave April a kiss on the top of her head.

"OK then, but I'm going to have to report this you know".

"That's fine" Brook said _"we'll be waiting for your call"_ as she gave him a kiss on the cheek then left the bus.

"Have a safe trip back to where you're going" the bus driver smiled as he closed the door.

"Now to get you home and back into our loving arms" April smiled as they turned the car around and headed for home.

"Yes where you can stay for as long as you want, for my place is now your place and that goes for you two as well" looking at Lexie and April.

Jake was to awake the next morning in one hell of a sticky mess, as he realized that nothing had changed. He was still the same old Jake that he was the night before. He didn't have a handy men job, he didn't have the care of three very lovely ladies; nor did he live on some big estate. All he had to live in was some run down old apartment and he was still unemployed for it had been _**All in a Dream**_.

www.ingramcontent.com/pod-product-compliance
Lightning Source LLC
Chambersburg PA
CBHW040544170726
48295CB00012B/590